EMPIRE'S END
A ROMAN STORY

Empire's End
A ROMAN STORY

LEILA RASHEED

Series Consultant:

Tony Bradman

■SCHOLASTIC

In hope of peace in Libya.

Scholastic Children's Books,
Euston House, 24 Eversholt Street, London NW1 1DB, UK
A division of Scholastic Ltd

London ~ New York ~ Toronto ~ Sydney ~ Auckland
Mexico City ~ New Delhi ~ Hong Kong

First published in the UK by Scholastic Ltd, 2019

ISBN 978 1407 19139 3

Printed and bound by CPI Group (UK) Ltd, Croydon, CR0 4YY

2 4 6 8 10 9 7 5 3 1

www.scholastic.co.uk

1.

BURYING THE PAST

On a clear day, you can see to the end of the Empire from here.

It has taken us all morning to ride from our farm up to the top of the cliffs that look out over the harsh northern sea. I'm glad of the two little Silurian ponies we bought last year. Without them, it would be an even longer journey. Even so, I'm tired by the time we get to the cliffs. The wind whips my pony's rough mane against my skin. It draws stinging tears to my eyes.

Ahead of me on the other pony, you don't seem to notice the wind. Perhaps you're too young to feel pain. Yet you're sprouting up so fast! I'm used to the speed of growing apple

1

trees and wheat, but the speed a human grows at – that's a surprise to me. Every year takes you further out of danger; not that we'd ever say that aloud and tempt the gods. The little burial ground near our farm holds too many babies who never breathed and too many little ones their parents had only just dared to name. Nothing is more dangerous out here, near the end of the Empire, than being a child.

At the edge of the cliff, I rein in my pony and look out to sea. The sea is hardly ever blue here. Sometimes it glints as brightly as the silver box I have strapped to my saddle. But not today. Today the sea is dark as thunderclouds.

The silver box, too, will turn dark without my careful hands to polish it every day. It was a gift from an empress – the most powerful woman in the world. Even so, I have outlived her and all her heirs. The box already looks as if it comes from a vanished world.

Your shouts mingle with seagulls' cries as you canter back and forth, pretending to be a chariot-warrior. You urge your pony down the steep slope, halt it, turn it back again. You have no fear. You don't know what there is to be afraid of. I itch to tell you to be careful, but I hold my tongue. You need to be fearless. It is a hard life in Britain. No place for cowards.

"Hail Caesar!" you yell, and wave your spear above your head. I smile; you see nothing strange in moving from playing at British charioteers to saluting the Roman Emperor. That's your life: one minute you're a Roman centurion, primus *pilus even, the very best soldier of all, and the next you're Vercingetorix leading the rebels against the Empire. Your blue eyes come from your Brigante grandmother, but your warm smile is just like your Libyan grandfather's. I wonder who your children, my grandchildren, will look like. I wonder where they will play, and if I will live to see them. At least I will do my best to leave them something to remember me by: this silver box of memories.*

"We should go down to the ruins now," I tell you. Obedient, you follow me as I ride down the slope. The fallen stone walls have been here so long that the grass has grown over them. We wouldn't know they were here, if years ago I hadn't cut a slice of turf and found that the things I thought were rocks were actually the remains of walls.

The path down is steep. I dismount and lead the pony after me. Once we are in the hollow, no one can see us. We are hidden from the sea. I think, perhaps, if we had been seafaring folk, things might be different. But we are not. We are farmers. We can't sail away when things get hard.

The turf has already been cleared. Arcturus did that a few days ago, last time he came to look. He said the ruins were not built by the Brigantes, his mother's tribe. He said they were much older than that. He said to keep them a secret, because they could come in useful one day.

One day. We have been thinking of that day, planning for it, since before you were born. But, on the night of the last full moon, I was sure. Now is the time to bury our treasures – in case we have to leave home, fast.

I lift the box down from the pony's back. It is wrapped in an old cloth, to shield it from prying eyes. The things inside are my treasures, not your father's. I know them off by heart.

A prayer for a child's safety, written on papyrus grown at the other side of the Empire.

A gold ring inscribed with two Greek letters: chi and rho.

A scrap of blue silk stained by seawater.

A bracelet of black jet from British shores.

A small golden pot with a lid made to look like a coiled snake: red glass eyes and shining scales, a diamond on its head.

They have all come so far with me. I refuse to lose them now. Instead, I'll bury them here. Maybe one day we'll feel safe enough to dig them up again, and I can tell the stories properly, around the fire as stories should be told.

I unwrap the silver box for a last look at it. On the lid, there are snakes curling around a staff. It is the staff of Asclepius, the god of medicine and healing. My family have always worshipped him. On the sides, Hercules and Dionysus: gods of the distant east. Dionysus rides a panther. I saw one once, in a cage. I will never forget how its eyes burned like suns. Even on this cold, shivery day I can still feel the ghost of heat from that memory.

"Can we go now?" you say, fidgeting.

4

I place the box into the earth and pack the turf down around it. "We will come back," I whisper, and I say a short prayer to the spirits of this place, whoever they are. "I promise we will come back."

It is as we ride up out of the small valley that you spot them. Your eyes are sharper than mine.

"Sails!" you yell, and point to the water.

My heart skips like a stone skimmed across water – then sinks. They are not Roman sails; just the fishing boats. We know these men. I raise a hand in greeting.

But you have already seen my expression.

"Mother," you say, "why do you fear the sea?"

I fear the sea because enemies come from the sea, I think. But I don't want to scare you.

"Oh, just because a long time ago, I was caught in a storm," I say.

"Like when Jupiter's Oak got hit by lightning?" you say, meaning a year ago when a great tree we've always used as a landmark was struck. You had nightmares about the blaze for a long time afterwards.

"Yes, but worse, because this time the storm was at sea."

"Storms at sea are not scary," you say. "You don't have to go out and bring the animals to shelter. There's nothing to get burned out there."

I remember that you have only ever seen a storm at sea as something far off; spears of light jabbing the shield of the water.

5

You have only ever felt grateful that it stays out there and does not come on to land.

"Unless you're on board a ship," I say.

"You were on board a ship?" you say. "In a storm? What was that like?"

I never meant to start telling the story like this, here and now. But as we ride on, I realise that some stories are so big, that, like the ocean, if you think too hard about it you'll never start swimming. You just have to take a deep breath and jump in. In medias res, my father would say: right in the middle of the thing. Jump in, and hope you can swim your way out again.

So as we ride homewards, the huge sea at our back, I take a deep breath and dive into the story.

208 AD

2.

THE HEART OF
THE STORM

I wanted to die.

The captain had sent all the passengers below decks when the waves got so high that even the strongest of us could not keep our footing. We had been stuck in our cabin for so long I had lost count of the time. I could hear my father and mother coughing and retching near me. For a long time we had lain in our bunks, sick and shivering with terror, listening to the shouts of the sailors on deck and the ship creaking and groaning all around us.

"I feel like a British Druid," my father had moaned, once the ship started pitching as well as rolling, "wrapped up in a bull's hide for thirty days and thirty nights until I start to sweat poetry."

That was the last thing any of us said for a while. We were too ill and frightened to talk, and the ship was being tossed around so much that we could not stand up. It was pitch black except for the flicker of lightning. There was no chance of a lamp in this storm; the flame would only have set light to the ship. Outside the thunder crashed and the wind howled so loud we could no longer hear the captain and the sailors. Every time we rose up on the crest of a wave, I clung to the edge of my bunk, and every time we crashed down again, I thought the ship would break apart around me.

We were supposed to have been in Britain already. It was supposed to be a short trip across the Mare Britannicum, the strip of sea that separated Gaul and Britain. The fleet had set sail on a fine spring day, with a good wind. It should have taken barely two days to get there. Instead, a few hours into the journey, the first clouds started forming in the sky. I could not believe how fast they moved, like an iron-clad legion closing in on us.

Rolled about in my bunk, like dice in a hand, I no longer believed in Britain. I was so ill and so delirious that I actually thought it was a lie as so many had said in the beginning; a legendary place of monsters; a dream island that vanished into Hell as soon as you seemed likely to set foot on it. I certainly didn't believe I would get there. I didn't believe I'd get anywhere except to the bottom of the sea, where there was no wind and no waves and I was just bones which couldn't vomit any more.

Thoughts chased each other madly around my head like charioteers around the Circus Maximus. I knew Neptune was angry when there was a storm, but I couldn't understand why he was so angry with *me*. I was just a fourteen-year-old girl. What could I possibly have done? *Perhaps*, I thought, *it's not me the gods are angry with but some hero whose ship's path has crossed mine. Maybe I am caught up in the flailing tail of someone else's story. Perhaps*, I thought, *I had better try to get up and pray – ask the gods for mercy.*

My father's hand grasped mine just as I thought that. I realised he was saying my name, over and over again: "Camilla! Camilla!" And then: "Have to get out!"

My mother grasped my other hand, and they pulled me from my bunk. I was in water, first up to my ankles, then my knees. My father led us towards the steps leading up to the deck – not that easy when the floor did not stay still. By the time we had fumbled our way in darkness to the door, my skirts were swimming around me.

My father forced the door open. A gust of wind took it and slammed it off its hinges, and a wave crashed down the steps and into the cabin. As I stepped out of the cabin, something heavy slammed into my wrist, and my mother's hand suddenly slipped from mine. I was left clinging to my father on the flooded deck.

"Ma!" I screamed. I turned back, but I could not see her anywhere. There was just broken wood, tossed on the water, and lightning-lit waves crashing down on us. I realised our ship was not just sinking – it had already sunk, the deck was below the water, and the waves were tearing it apart like a wild beast tearing at a hunk of meat.

"Ma!" I tried to scream again, but this time I choked on a mouthful of water. Then I was in the sea, and my feet were kicking water, not wooden boards. In the lightning flashes, I could see other ships, rearing up like monsters around us.

I knew how to swim. My father had insisted that I learn, that my mother take me to the baths in the morning and let me work out how to paddle myself along. But a warm bath in Leptis Magna was not a freezing cold storm in the Mare Britannicum. I kicked out towards the ships and sank straight down, my dress tangled around my legs like hateful seaweed.

Stay alive, I told myself as I sank into cold, roaring green water with no bottom to it. *Stay alive. Alive. Alive.*

That is all I remember.

Later, my father told me that we were picked up by a ship from the Classis Britannica, the troop-carriers that ferry soldiers across from Gaul. Those of us who escaped the wreck huddled shivering, caked with salt, on the deck of the ship that had rescued us. The Emperor's ship had survived the storm and sailed on to Londinium ahead of us. We were ordered to follow.

After the storm, pieces of our lives were laid out across the calm sea. They floated gently, bobbing up and down, silent survivors. It was as if the gods had fought like squabbling toddlers, snatched what they wanted, then tossed the unwanted toys away. We rescued a crate of drowned chickens, a barrel of fresh water. We pulled shoes and sailcloth from the sea. We pulled bodies from the sea too, bodies who had been people: Callirhoe, the freedwoman whose sharp tongue everyone on board had feared; the twin slave boys who used to bicker all the time and would now be silent forever; Fortuna, a jolly old woman, who had been making her first sea journey, to join her daughter's family in Londinium. And those were just the ones I recognised.

We wrapped them all in sailcloth and said prayers over them and tried to comfort their families. Those of us who had survived swapped stories of the horror and the miracles: the Emperor's chef, from Gaul, with a waistline fattened on wild boar, had survived by clinging to a barrel of his favourite Falernian wine.

We never found my mother. That blow that separated her hand from mine was the last we ever knew of her.

"It was the will of the gods," my father said to me as the mouth of the river drew into sight. In just a few days he had grown a grizzled beard, and his face was all shadows and hollows. "If Aeneas can bear it, so can we."

He fell silent. Aeneas, the founder of Rome, escaped from the destruction of Troy but lost his wife, Creusa, on the way through the burning city. Every Roman child knew this story off by heart. I knew it as well as anyone. Aeneas, a Trojan prince, wakes to find that the Greeks have tricked their way into his city and are burning it down around him. He tries to get his family – his wife, Creusa, his old father and his baby son – to safety. But on the way out, he realises Creusa is no longer following him. He turns back to look for her. He desperately searches the city, and finds Creusa – but only her ghost, which slips through his arms when he tries to hug her.

That story, too, starts with a storm at sea.

I never told my father, but I used to imagine that Creusa had really escaped and lived on, hidden somewhere from the Greeks. There were hardly any girls or women in the story of Aeneas, after all. But there was no way my mother could have survived the shipwreck. I knew I had to be a brave Roman woman and accept the will of the gods, but within, I felt as hollow as a bronze statue.

Just before we entered the mouth of the river to sail up to Londinium, a sailor spotted a chest floating on the water. When we hauled it up, it was dripping and already growing barnacles. It turned out to be ours. Inside was my mother's best blue silk stola. She had bought it just before we went to Rome. We had never seen a dress made of cloth as thin and fine as this. It was like touching a dream. The saleswoman who brought it to our house was full of stories of how it had taken four years to bring it over land and sea from another empire at the far end of the world. When she finally mentioned the price, my mother dropped it as if it were hot, but my father said, "We are going to Rome now, you must dress like a woman of quality," and he bought it for her. I think she was more pleased than she liked to show.

The stola was almost all ruined by seawater, but I tore off a piece that rippled like the sea itself. It still smelled of her. I buried my face in it and closed my eyes and tried to imagine that she was there. I felt like Aeneas, trying to hold onto a ghost.

"You must be strong, daughter," my father said to me gently. "Death comes when it is time for it to come.

To everything its season. Let us not wish for figs in winter."

But I did wish for figs. As our ship sailed slowly upriver into Britain, the loneliest and bleakest province of the Empire, I longed – more than I longed for anything except to hear my mother's voice again – for sweet, juicy fresh figs: a taste of my home that was so far away.

I glance over at you as we ride down the hill. You're only seven. Too young for this sad story, perhaps. Your face is serious.

"I don't understand. Why did you even come to Britain?" you say. "Why not stay in Rome, where you were born?"

"I was not born in Rome!" I say. "Don't you know that? I was born in Leptis Magna."

"Leptis Magna?" You shrug. "Where's that?"

That's it, then. I have no choice but to tell you the whole story. Sad and scary as it may be, you have to know where you come from. So I go on. But I choose my words carefully, as if I'm hopping over rocks at the beach, avoiding the slippery dangerous bits.

3.

A City of Gold

I wasn't born in Rome. I was born in the city of
Leptis Magna, part of the province of Libya. My
father's family were from Rome, but my mother's
family had lived in Leptis Magna since long before
the Romans ruled it. We spoke Punic at home, but we
read Latin and Greek – and I dreamed in a mixture
of all three.

Leptis Magna perches on the north shore of Africa.
It is one of a chain of merchant cities, like Berenice and
Apollonia, that got rich on buying and selling. Its gods
are Hercules and Dionysus. It's a city of gold: golden

sunlight, golden sandstone and golden coins changing hands in the marketplace.

I was born in the Year of the Five Emperors, and all my life, things had been good in Leptis Magna. The fifth and final emperor – Septimius Severus – who had come to power after the civil wars, had been born in Leptis Magna and he had poured wealth into the city. We had a new triumphal arch, a new basilica, a new forum, new public baths. Tourists came to admire the city that had produced a man brave and clever and ruthless enough to win at the game of power. My father's greatest boast – and he had plenty of boasts – was that he played marbles with the Emperor when they were boys. He said that even then, Septimius loved winning. It was no surprise when he went off to glory and conquests and my father turned his mind to philosophy and the science of medicine and the arts of Asclepius.

Once, my father took me to see the Emperor's triumphal arch. I was his only living child, and he was quite old, so he treated me more like a boy than he might have done otherwise.

The arch that Septimius Severus had had built to celebrate his victories over the Parthians had taken most of my lifetime to complete. It was enormous – you could see it looming over the city from a long way away, blinding white marble against the cloudless blue sky.

It had four entries, and sat over the crossroads, so that people coming from all sides of the city saw it.

"This arch is the heart of the city," my father announced proudly. "Every distance from Leptis Magna is measured from this point. When we say it is one hundred miles to Leptis Magna, we mean it is one hundred miles to this spot."

Awed, I craned back to try and see it all. Up the sides of the arch, the sculptor had carved coiling grapevines, the symbol of Dionysus who protected our city. There were barbarians, too, on the pillars, with strange clothes and long hair, looking sad and noble and strong.

The Emperor Septimius Severus was right in the centre of the highest panel. He was in a chariot, flanked by his two sons, Bassianus – who was always called Caracalla – and Geta. As I looked at the sculpture I could almost hear the roaring cheers of the crowd as they drove through Rome. It looked as if they were driving the chariot right out from the arch, trampling over the heads of everyone below them. Winged spirits of victory soared over their heads, dropping crowns of sacred palm leaves onto them.

"He looks like one of us," my father said with pride. And he did. He was curly-haired, with a dark face like a fighter, scarred like a dry riverbed by the sun. You could see men just like him setting out to fish from the port of Leptis Magna, or striding down to the baths in the afternoon. Of course, now that he was emperor, everyone *tried* to look like him even if they did not, but even so, he was clearly a son of Libya. I looked up at the next panel. Dignified and calm, the Emperor grasped the hands of his sons, Caracalla and Geta, who stood beside him. The folds of their togas made them look as solid and safe as three tall stone pillars.

"It is a great thing that the Emperor has sons to rule after him," remarked my father.

"Why?"

"Well, no one wants to go back to the days of the Year of the Five Emperors," he said. "You were born in that year, you would not know, but the Empire was torn apart by generals fighting for power."

I could not imagine it. I had known peace all my life.

"Caracalla and Geta will rule together after the Emperor becomes a god," my father said.

Becomes a god? That means when he dies, I realised. But you did not speak of the Emperor's death in public. People would think you were wishing him dead – perhaps that you were even plotting his death.

"Who was that meant to be?" I asked, to change the subject. I pointed at a man's figure that stood near to the Emperor. He was also carved in a toga, the folds of stone flowing down. But his head had been sheared off, as if by an axe blow.

My father sounded uncomfortable for the first time.

"Oh... that was Plautianus. He was a childhood friend of the Emperor, too."

"Did you know him? It's a pity his statue has been damaged. Will it be fixed?"

"I doubt it," said my father. Then, as if wanting to speak of something different, he said: "How do you think the stones of the arch stay up?"

I had never wondered that before. Now I found myself worrying, because I couldn't see how they were supported.

"Some sort of wire inside...?" I suggested, though I could not imagine what wire could be strong enough to hold up stone. Some of my mother's jewellery was made of gold wire but it was easy to crumple even just with clumsy fingers.

He shook his head.

I looked and looked. I felt as if there must be a secret in plain view.

After a moment, he told me the secret. "They hold each other up. Do you see? The force of each one holds its neighbours up."

"So if one were to be taken out..."

"The whole arch would fall down."

As we walked away I craned my neck to look back at the arch. I think my father meant me to be impressed at the skill of the engineers and I was, but I was now more worried that one day, one of the stones would be removed.

My mother was not a fan of the new Leptis Magna.

"I liked it better before," she grumbled quietly, when I came home with stories of how magnificent our new city was.

"I love it right now!" I said proudly. "Soon we will be just like Rome."

"Daddy's girl," said my father, and ruffled my hair.

It was true, I was a Daddy's girl. I read the books he told me to: Virgil and Cicero and Marcus Aurelius the philosopher-emperor, and even some books that my mother wasn't to know about, like Galen, the famous doctor. My lyre playing was best not spoken of (or heard), but my geometry was getting better and I was proud of knowing Latin and Greek as well as Punic.

"Now," my mother would say, if I ever sounded a bit too pleased with myself, "you have nothing left to do but find a husband who will put up with all this learning."

That always stopped my mouth quickly, because I could never imagine wanting to marry – even though, on the day the news came, I was already fourteen years old.

That day, I had just finished my morning lessons. My tutor – a Greek who taught me and a few other girls together, for a discounted rate – was putting away his writing materials, and my friend Livia and I were playing with the kittens that had been born that spring. They were just old enough to play now with strings and a little ball, chasing it, patting and padding it, and sometimes they would try to catch the fish that swam in the small pool in the *impluvium* where the rainwater collected in the spring. My mother was out shopping, and my father was giving a public demonstration of surgery in front of the house. We could hear his voice droning on, like bees around flowers. It was sunny, and the ground was warm under our bare feet. Now I often wake up dreaming of that sunshine, crying for it. I hunger for it the way I hunger for my mother's touch.

My old nurse was keeping an eye on us, and carding wool, combing and cleaning it as she sat in the shade, her wide lap holding the wool that still smelled of sheep. My mother would later spin the yarn to make clothes for my father and me. Nurse was from the tribe of the Garamantes, the ones who know where the wells and the secret gardens are and how to ride a camel from one side of the waterless desert to the other with only the stars to guide you. She had been enslaved when she was only a girl – not by us, we bought her from a neighbour – and she did not have the faded blue lines that mapped the faces of the other Garamantes women. She would watch them when they were in the market as if she was watching marvellous dreams she longed to enter. Now that she was old, past forty, and I was no longer a child, she wasn't my nurse any more. Still, I loved her more than my own mother. My mother was not unkind, but she only spoke to me to give me annoying advice or tell me what I was doing wrong. The long hours spent spinning or weaving or doing some other dutiful household task with my mother made me so bored I could have torn my own hair out. With Nurse, I could be sure of someone who would listen and smile no matter what I babbled about. Today, as so often, I was babbling about my mother and how annoying she was.

"My mother is so nervous these days," I was saying to Livia. "It's as if she is expecting bad news."

"Perhaps she is."

"Well, whether she is or not, she shouldn't let it show." Remembering something my father often said, I added, feeling rather smug, "Marcus Aurelius said that we should treat bad news and good news exactly the same—"

"Now, miss, don't speak ill of your mother, whatever the philosophers say. You don't know the whole story," interrupted Nurse gently.

"Really?" said Livia, who had recently started acting a little like her own mother: suddenly on her dignity, cold. "What secrets do you think your mistress has, and why would it concern you?"

"Did I say secrets, miss?" she replied.

I gave Livia a little push, uncomfortable at the direction in which she was steering things.

At the time, though, I did think that Nurse meant secrets. I knew that my parents had secrets from me already. I had seen the messengers from Rome come and go in the night, and spotted the pigeons that my father sent flying across the sea. Girls aren't supposed to ask questions about such things, but you can't have a father who believes in philosophy and education for girls and not end up with a curious mind. Sometimes I thought, guiltily, that my father had probably only meant me to learn how I should behave as a good Roman woman: brave, chaste, choosing death before dishonour. I was sure he wouldn't want me wondering about his private business. The trouble was, all those stories of good Roman women seemed a little distant. I didn't need to choose death before dishonour and there were no wars for me to be brave in; even the Garamantes were peaceful these days... What really worried me then was that Livia would choose to make a big scandal out of Nurse's words, and my mother would have to say she would have Nurse whipped, so as not to lose face in front of Livia's mother. Of course, we would never whip an old slave, but I cringed at the thought of having to *pretend* we had.

Then the kitten fell into the *impluvium*, and the panic over getting it out before it drowned made us all forget what we were talking about. I remember noticing that the voices from the surgery demonstration had stopped. Now there was silence when before there had been constant, reassuring noise. It was as if someone had taken the sea away.

"Poor little thing," we crooned over the kitten. We dried it carefully – it had only been in the water a few seconds – and took it back to its mother for something to drink in the sun. But when we came back, the atmosphere had changed. Nurse was gone, my father was there, and from one look at him I could see that he was near bursting with news. His eyes were shining like marble in the sun. I was amazed. I had never seen him look so excited and happy.

"Father?" I said.

"Camilla!" He took my shoulder and smiled – no, grinned – into my face. "Come on, I have news."

I followed him, full of excitement, into his office. We did not have the wealthiest house in the city, but it was homely, and my mother had made sure we had the most up-to-date painters to decorate the dining room with scenes of the labours of Hercules and Dionysus riding on a panther. The office was a room I rarely went into. My father's wooden desk was there, with a stack of letters and writing tablets and, in the corner, his seal and wax. There was also a screen carved out of scented cedar wood, and a mural of Mercury, messenger of the gods, who was a good choice for business. A bust of the Emperor in pink marble was in a niche on the wall, and there were some elegant folding chairs for guests. My mother was already in the room, looking worried as usual.

My father shut the doors, closing us in the cool shade, and turned to us.

"It has happened. Finally!" he burst out.

I stared at him, confused, but my mother's face fell.

"You mean—" she began.

"Yes! The Emperor has summoned me to Rome! We are going home!"

4.

GOING HOME

"We're leaving Leptis Magna?" my mother said.

I was confused. Home was here – this villa, this courtyard, those kittens, the comfortable feel of the mosaic floor beneath my feet.

My father grasped my hands and spoke directly to me. "You know I lived in Rome as a young man. Well, the Emperor has finally remembered his childhood friend! He has called for me personally. We are going back to Rome – to the centre of the world, Camilla! The only place that matters!"

"Rome!" I was thrilled. I squeezed my father's hands. I had never been to Rome; I'd only heard people talk of it. If they had been there they sounded lordly and superior, and if they had not they spoke of it with longing and jealousy. Rome – the centre of the world!

The home of the Emperor himself! The heart of the Empire!

My mother had found a smile by now. Her next words took mine away.

"At last, we can conclude things with Publius," she said to my father. "It will be a joy to me to see my daughter honourably and safely settled."

I dropped my father's hands.

"You mean *marry*? Me, marry?" I said.

My mother smiled at me.

"You will finally be a grown woman," she said softly. "We are so proud."

I nodded uncertainly. I knew, of course, that I was engaged to be married. So was Livia, and so were most of my friends. I had a ring that my mother kept in a box in her room, which I had been given as a betrothal token. But the boy – Publius Maecenas – was in Rome, so far away, or so it had seemed until now. I had assumed that the engagement had been forgotten, that when I married it would be someone from Leptis Magna. We had met just once, when his family had visited Leptis Magna for the betrothal ceremony when I was only six. But now I was fourteen. I didn't remember him at all. I searched my memory and came up with a vague idea of soft brown eyes, freckles and knobbly elbows.

28

"Fourteen is young," said my father, as if reading my mind. "But at least you can get to know each other."

I realised, the thought flying through my mind like a swallow dipping in and out of the eaves, that this was what all the messages, the secrets, had been leading up to. This invitation to Rome had not come out of nowhere. My father had been working towards it, perhaps begging the Emperor to invite him, perhaps speaking to others who had the Emperor's ear, just as I wheedled my mother's maid when I wanted some little toy or jewel and my mother was doubtful. And the end of it was that we were all going to Rome.

And I was going to get married.

"His family are well-born and rich," my mother said. "It is a good marriage for a doctor's daughter from the provinces."

"You forget that we are friends of the Emperor," my father replied. "Being from the provinces is no longer a disadvantage, when the Emperor himself speaks Latin with a Leptis Magna accent."

Married, I thought. I would be a grown woman. With a household of my own. That didn't sound so bad. Still, I had a thousand thoughts and fears. What would it be like being married? Would I enjoy being a grown woman? And what about, well... having babies? What if – an even more worrying thought – I could *not* have babies? I knew some women could not, and it seemed to make them very sad, for they spent much time and money coming to my father and then going to different temples and even sailing to faraway places where the gods had been said to work miracles. If I could not have children, what would I do all day? Would my husband divorce me? I realised that I had gone from not thinking of Publius at all to marrying him and divorcing him in less than a minute.

"Can I go on with my studies?" I asked my father.

He patted my head. "Yes, of course. There is no need for you to marry in a rush. Take your time. See how you like each other. I expect you will like each other very much!"

"It is best for girls to marry early," my mother said gently. "She is nearly fifteen after all."

"The philosophers disagree," my father replied, and my mother could say no more.

I skipped out to tell Nurse the news.

"We're going to Rome! Rome itself!"

Nurse was bending over the basket of wool, and she didn't look up. I was disappointed.

"Nurse! Didn't you hear? We're all going to Rome! You too!"

When she did look up, I searched her face for the excitement I expected her to feel. I did not find it.

30

"Nurse?" I said uncertainly.

"To Rome?" she said, and her voice sounded blank and empty. "Must I go to Rome?"

"Of course!" I laughed aloud. "Of course you must come to Rome with us. We would not leave you here."

I flung my arms around her neck and hugged her. She had fed me as a baby, put me to sleep every night. She had even given me a little amulet, a spell written on papyrus and contained in a reed, which I wore tied around my wrist all the time. It was a good-luck spell from a priest of Isis, meant to keep me safe from illness. Every time I looked at it, it reminded me of how much she loved me.

"I'm going to be married," I whispered into her ear. The amulet dug into my wrist as I hugged her. "You can come and live with me in my new house, in Rome. It's the greatest city in the world!"

Then I ran off to give thanks to our household gods, our Lares and Penates. Their familiar shrine was in the entrance hall, and we went every day, to speak to the warm, loving spirits who watched over us. I did not look back, because I was a little bit scared that Nurse was not happy about the news, and I did not want to think about that. There was no way I was going to go to Rome, marry a stranger and live in a strange house without Nurse by my side.

31

5.

CHILDHOOD'S END

Livia was jealous. She pretended she was sad to lose me, but she tore my nicest dress and said it was an accident, and she took delight in giving Nurse petty, humiliating orders in front of me. I did not dare say anything to her. Her family was wealthier than ours, and she was used to being in charge, and besides she was older than me. She wanted to know about Publius, though.

"Is he handsome? Is he very old?"

I shrugged. "I think he's about twenty. I don't know if he is handsome." I didn't like talking about Publius, because there were so many things I didn't know and couldn't find out. Besides, my mother had become even more nervous now that we were preparing to leave. She kept me inside most of the day, sewing and weaving. It was as if she was afraid I would do something to disgrace us all before I got to Rome. "Now you are soon to be married," she kept on saying, "things are different."

My reading became extremely boring, and also worrying. There was no more *Aeneid*; instead there were endless stories about how to be a good wife and mother. I was ready to learn about how to be a perfect Roman woman, but I did wonder why so many of them had to die in the end.

"I wish I *was* married," I complained to Livia. "I'd be my own mistress then." The more I had to sit inside on days when it was sunny outside, the more I couldn't wait to get to Rome.

"The Emperor has two sons," said Livia thoughtfully. "You could marry one of them."

I wrinkled my nose. "I think they're even older than Publius."

"So?" Livia picked up Lucia, my wooden doll, the one I hadn't played with for a long time now. Lucia had long, slim limbs that really moved, and womanly curves. We had spent hours, Livia and I, playing at households and shopping with our dolls. We had visited Rome a thousand times in games. We had made clothes for them with scraps of our own old clothes. Now, Livia turned Lucia back and forth, like a noblewoman looking over a potential slave girl.

"You should give your childhood dolls to Venus," Livia told me. "It's the elegant thing to do."

I didn't really want to give Lucia away, even to a goddess. But after I had shown off about becoming a grown-up married lady, I felt I had to. Besides, it would get me out of the house for once. My mother listened, then nodded: the idea pleased her.

"I am glad you are accepting childhood is over," she said. "You are of the age when you should be married – whatever the philosophers say. You need a household of your own, and some children to keep you busy."

I wasn't sure about that, but at least I was going outside.

"You can come with me to the temple," I told Nurse. "You will enjoy that, won't you? You have never seen the temple of Venus."

Nurse smiled at me. There seemed a shadow in her eyes though, and she moved more slowly these days, as if carrying a heavy weight. But I had no time to worry about her as the days went on and my father began to arrange our passage to Rome. A whole household – all of us, and our belongings, and our slaves – had to be packed up. The horses were sold and the hens, too. I cried when the horses were taken away. I loved them.

"Perhaps I can have a horse when I am married," I said to Livia.

Livia snorted.

"Horses are only for men. Roman women do not ride – they are carried, like precious treasures."

The only creatures that still hung around the courtyard were the stray cats. Last year's kittens were young toms now. Late in the night the brothers wailed and squalled and slashed each other's ears with their sharp claws, fighting over territory, until someone forced themself to get out of bed and sling a sandal and a string of curses at them.

One evening, the moment I had quietly dreaded arrived.

"Miss," Nurse began. She was at the door of my bedroom. "May I speak to you?"

I knew she had come to see me especially, and chosen a moment my parents were both busy at the opposite end of the house. I feared what she was going to say, so I began talking quickly, trying to pretend she was not going to say it.

"Of course, Nurse!" I rushed. "I am so looking forward to going to Rome! They say that everyone must see it once before they die. Aren't you excited, Nurse? I'm so excited for you! Just think, who could have known you would be lucky enough to see Rome?

You know Livia said we should sell you before we leave, but I said I would never sell you; I want you with me forever. I may have children some day and then you could look after them too and we would be so happy, wouldn't we? So happy!"

I went on like this for a long time. I can hardly bear to remember it. She waited for me to stop talking, but I didn't. I wouldn't. And in the end, because my throat was getting dry, I said: "I'm so sorry, Nurse, I have to go, my mother is calling me."

There was a pause as we both listened to the complete silence, and then she smiled sadly, and nodded, and stepped back into the shadows.

In the end, there was so much to do that it was not until the day before we were due to take ship for Rome that my mother had time to take me to dedicate Lucia to Venus at the temple. The night before, I folded Lucia's best dresses, thinking how long I had spent making them, imagining the day I would be a woman myself and have dresses like these. My heart beat fast. It made me feel a little sick to think that tomorrow, Lucia would be gone forever – gone to the goddess of love. It did not matter that it was years since I had played with her. She was leaving me. I would be alone. Grown up. A woman. The future looked as dark and mysterious as the sea at night, with only a dim path of moonlight, and shadows everywhere else.

"Look after her, Venus," I whispered. It took me a long time to fall asleep.

When I woke up, I thought at once of Nurse. I would need her to help me get ready. I opened the door but she was not sleeping outside as she usually was.

"Nurse," I called, but she did not come. Annoyed at her laziness – today of all days – I hurried to get myself dressed. When I needed my hair brushed I came out again to look for her. But she was not there.

My mother was looking for me, flustered. No one had seen Nurse, but there was no time to hunt for her. We had to hurry to the temple. My mother's slave girl did my hair, and we went out in the litter – our hand-carried chair – together. My mother insisted on a closed litter, for her usual reason: "Now that you are soon to be married."

Behind the curtains of the litter, it was stuffy. I could not see the streets, except glimpses as the curtains swayed. I could smell things though: donkeys and goats, the fishmongers, baking bread and the vinegary sharp smell of wine and pickles. And garum: my favourite, salty fish sauce that made everything taste better. *On a horse,* I thought, *I would be able to see far above people's heads.*

We took a long time to get to the temple, for there were errands my mother needed to run on the way, but at last we arrived. A group of worshippers were already there. Some were girls, like me, with dolls in their hands. We glanced at each other shyly, but there was no time to make friends. Before I knew it, I had laid my doll on the altar of Venus. There was the smell of incense and a priestess recited prayers, and we were moved on – after my mother had given a donation, of course, for the temple roof. My prayer had gone to Venus, along with Lucia and her six dresses that I had sewn together with my own clumsy hands. The next clothes I sewed would be real clothes for real children, I realised. The thought made my stomach feel as if caged birds were fluttering all around inside it.

My mother kept me close to her as we left the temple and returned to our waiting litter. I almost wanted to cry. I felt a little foolish, let down by the day and nervous about the future. Most of all, I felt angry with Nurse, for not being there, for being missing on the very first day I was grown up. I thought of all the cruel, stern, reproachful things I would say to her when I got back.

But when I got back, she was not there.

By the evening, it was clear – unbelievably – that she had run away.

*

"Someone has stolen her," I said to my father. "Nurse would never run away. This is her home."

He looked at me with pity, but shook his head. "Who would steal an old woman? No, it's clear she has gone. She picked a good day to run, knowing we would be sailing the next day. I will send out messengers and when she is caught she will be returned to Livia's family, who will deal with her."

"But – what will happen to her?"

"She has run away. They will have to whip her or brand her."

"No!"

"Camilla, if we do not, what is to stop every slave from doing the same?"

"But not Nurse!"

My father took my hand and led me to the window. From the window of his study we could look down towards the busy city and the marketplace.

"You remember how we admired the arch that Septimius Severus gave to us?" said my father to me. "Do you remember how it stands up? I told you."

I shook my head. I did remember, but I didn't want to.

"It stands up because every stone remains in its allotted place, and does not change its position. In the same way, being a Roman means keeping your place and doing your duty, even when it is hard," my father told me. "Out there, there are millions of slaves. They are in every household. They stay in their place because they respect the strength of Rome. The law says that if one slave kills his master, all the slaves in the household must be put to death, even if there are hundreds of them."

"That's. . . not fair!"

"It is Roman law. It is *our* law. We have peace, because our law works. We must show the world how Rome behaves to rebels, or every slave will rise up and destroy us. We did not ask to be Romans, but we are – and we must hold together."

There was nothing else for me to say. I cried in my room for the rest of the night.

How could Nurse have run off? I asked myself over and over again. How could she have been so ungrateful? I punched my cushion and pretended it was her. I would have broken my doll and pretended it was her, but Lucia was with Venus now.

None of it made a difference. The next day the weather was fair, and we set sail for Rome, as planned.

208 AD

6.

COLD MARBLE

We set sail from Leptis Magna on a hot spring day. The harbour was crowded with a consignment of panthers and lions for the games in Rome, and as soon as I heard the snarling from the cages and smelled the reek of them, all thoughts of Nurse were driven out of my head. Their eyes were as fierce as the sun itself – I couldn't look into them without blinking. I had never seen anything so golden. My mother went into a panic: what if they got loose on the ship?

But the crossing was calm and none of the beasts got loose. We could even wave to the other ships that were travelling alongside us. I saw my first dolphins, threading like silver needles through the sun-glittering sea, and the captain pointed out a plume of smoke from the island where the god Vulcan's forge was said to be. Mountains rose, blue shadows on the horizon. Veils of cloud hung over them. High up, beyond the clouds, in a bright, shining world, the gods lived. *Maybe Lucia was up there with Venus,* I thought to myself. And then we were in Italia: the home of the Romans, the heart of the Empire.

As soon as we reached dry land, we were flung into a confident, sweaty, bustle of people who all seemed to know where they were going. We must have stood out as new arrivals, because carriage drivers swarmed around us immediately.

"Bargain ride – direct to Rome!"

"Looking for a carriage? This is the fastest – you'll go like Mercury!"

I clung to my mother's hand, but my father, eyes gleaming, charged into the fray and came back with a carriage driver he swore was the best and cheapest of all. I wasn't sure about that, but I was just glad to get away from the port.

We travelled up the busy Appian Way. I peered through the window of the carriage, fascinated by the messengers galloping by on official business, the farmers

and slaves working in the fields. It all seemed so busy.
It was busy in Leptis too, but now I felt as if the place
I had come from was rough and crude. It was not so
much that the villas I glimpsed from the carriage were
finer and more magnificent than the ones in Leptis, or
that there were more of them. It was just that they had
a way of looking completely at home in the landscape,
as if they were safe.

Yes, safe. That was how it felt here – that we were
at the heart of the Empire, not on the borders. Look
wherever you wanted, you saw only Rome. It was hard
to believe that this was all under the control of someone
my father had once played marbles with. Even harder
to believe that in the year I was born, the Empire had
been in such chaos that it was sold off by its soldiers to
the highest bidder. I thought of Septimius Severus with
more awe and fear than I had ever done before. It was
as if we were going to meet Hercules or Dionysus.

My father had arranged for us to break the journey
with an old friend who was spending the summer in
one of these villas. We left the main road and followed a
path up the hill. Cypress trees cast long shadows over the
fields where some slaves were still toiling. I remembered
Nurse, and wondered where she was and if she was
safe. In the distance, sunlight flashed from metal and I
thought of hot metal burning, branding skin.

"What a beautiful house," my mother breathed, breaking into my sad thoughts.

The sun was setting, casting a pink and lilac glow over the villa and the vineyards that ran down the hill to the river. As we approached I could see my father's friend standing smiling and waiting for us under the portico. We stepped down from the carriage, rattled and tired and sweaty.

"Quintus Camillus, my friend!" the master of the house called out, and hurried to embrace my father. Lucius was a big, jolly man, whom my father would have diagnosed with an excess of yellow bile if he had met him in the street in Leptis Magna.

"Lucius!" My father's eyes were full of tears of joy. "And, Aemilia, you don't look a day older than when I last saw you."

Lucius' wife stepped forwards with a gracious smile. She was tall and dressed in silk, with gold and pearls around her neck and a jewelled ring for every slender finger. I felt travel-dusty and awkward, next to her.

"You're back from exile in the provinces!" Lucius clapped my father on the back.

"Finally," my father replied. "Back at the heart of things, where I should be."

"Ah, there is nowhere like Rome," Lucius said with a grin. "You have been away for so long – you

46

must hear the latest gossip. Did you know that the senate. . ."

They vanished into the depths of the house, leaving us with Lucius' wife.

"Your house is beautiful, Aemilia," said my mother.

"Oh, just a country villa, but we have a good site for it," she said modestly. "But come in, you must be so thirsty and hungry after your long journey!"

We went in and paid our respects to the family gods, Lares and Penates, in the entrance hall. As we walked into the courtyard, slaves came scurrying with bowls of rosewater and dried fruits. I tried not to stare, but it was impossible not to notice how comfortable, well-designed and carefully tended the house was. Water danced in fountains, cooling the air. Vines embraced the pillars, making shade from which ripe grapes hung down temptingly. If you glanced towards any window or arch, you were sure to see some especially beautiful bit of mountain or sea, framed as if in a picture. It was clear that it had all been planned to show off everything that was beautiful about the area. There were no stray cats slinking about, and although there were plenty of slaves, none of them were sitting by the *impluvium*, comfortably carding wool that still smelled of sheep. I swallowed, feeling homesick for our simpler world.

Aemilia looked at us with fascination as we washed our hands and politely nibbled the fruit.

"It must be so hard to live in the provinces," she murmured. "I hear it is complete desert in Libya – dry as a bone! With barbarians and wild beasts swarming everywhere!"

My mother and I opened our mouths at the same moment to protest.

"There are beautiful gardens in Leptis, and we too have green mountains," my mother said. "And our theatre has the most magnificent views of the sea."

"Really?" Aemilia was clearly not sure that Leptis Magna contained anything to match up to Rome. "Just one theatre? Poor you."

When we went for dinner, we were even more amazed. We had owned one bust of the Emperor. Here, in the *triclinium* alone, there were several, all in different colours of marble. Everywhere you looked were elegant bronze statues, or murals that looked like real life.

"So close to Rome, one can get anything," Aemilia said with a wave of her elegant, pale hand, ringed with cameos and gold. "Our next project is a new bathhouse."

"We have a bathhouse," grumbled Lucius.

"Yes, but it's so tired-looking – I hate setting foot

in there." Aemilia made a face. "So important to be up to date. I'm sure Camilla will agree?"

She smiled at me and I blushed. Not even Livia's family had a bathhouse of their own.

Even in this cool spring weather, when the sun had almost set, I noticed Aemilia did not step outside without a slave coming running to hold a parasol over her head. When her fingers brushed my arm, they felt like cool marble. For the first time ever, I felt as if my skin was coarse and sunburned. After all, in all the pictures of the imperial family, Julia Domna, the Empress, was shown with ivory-pale skin. I washed extra hard that evening, not that it made any difference. I was as brown as a man, as Aemilia had pointed out over dinner.

After Aemilia had left us alone in the bedroom we were to share, my mother removed her veil and shook the creases from it with surprising viciousness.

"Lucius and Aemilia are very kind," I ventured.

"A pity they did not show us some of this kindness when your father was banished," my mother replied. I was startled. It was the first time that I had ever heard her speak about that time.

"They did not protect us then. No one in Rome did," she added, then shut her lips tightly, as if she felt she had spoken too much.

49

"I thought you left Rome because of the troubles the year I was born?"

"No, your father was sent away before that. Some of the other doctors were jealous of his skill. They spoke ill of him to the Emperor Commodus. We were lucky he was not executed." She sighed. "Rome is a dangerous place."

We got ready for the night in silence. My mother unpacked our household gods and we said a quick prayer to them. It made me feel more at home, as if things were normal, and I decided I would do this every single night that I was away from home. Then I remembered that I would not be going home. If I married Publius, I would be staying in Rome. That thought sank like a heavy stone into my heart and lay there.

I lay awake. The room was the perfect temperature and the sheets a finer cotton than any we had ever slept on before. But it was hard to get used to the cooler air, and I ran over and over what my mother had said, trying to understand it. No one could stand up to imperial power, that was clear, so was it really fair to blame my father's friends for not defending him against the old emperor? Now Septimius Severus was emperor and we were in favour. There was really nothing to worry about – was there?

"We must be careful," my mother said aloud, into the darkness.

I turned over to face her. I could see only the outline of her face. The moonlight that came through the small window made everything look black and white.

"Why?"

"The Emperor's sons have a... bad reputation. They say Caracalla is like a wild beast. First he had his poor young wife, Plautilla, sent into exile. Then he had her father murdered. Plautianus was a powerful man, and he was the Emperor's friend from childhood, just as your father was. But Caracalla still had him put to death."

Plautianus. I remembered the headless carved figure on the arch that I had pointed out. The head had been sheared off as if with an executioner's axe. It seemed that if the Emperor wanted you dead, he did not just kill you – he killed all memory of you, too. No matter how powerful you might have been, he blasted you out of existence.

"But the Emperor will protect us, won't he?" I was wide awake now.

"I hope so..." She sighed. "I should not trouble you with this. Forget I said it. Your father has all the hopes – that leaves me with all the fears."

It was the first time, I realised, that I could

remember her saying anything to me that was not either a reproof or an instruction. It was the first time she had spoken to me as an adult and an equal, rather than a child. And even though what she had said was worrying, the heavy stone in my heart lightened a little. Perhaps being a married woman in Rome would not be so bad after all – not if my family stayed close to me.

We woke early, and were soon on our way to Rome. I looked back at the villa, feeling sorry to have to leave it so soon. It was so comfortable that even though Aemilia and Lucius might be untrustworthy, it was impossible not to feel as if you could stay there forever. Everyone seemed happy. My father had once told me to look at the slaves to judge the worth of a place. "If the slaves seem happy," he had said to me, "you can be sure that the household is a happy one."

And then I thought of Nurse again. She had seemed happy, but she had still run away.

7.

THE GREATEST CITY
IN THE WORLD

We found Rome guarded by the dead. Tombs lined the roads that led into the city. Beggars ran alongside us or called from the tombs, where some of them seemed to live. I was shocked. There were poor people in Leptis Magna too, of course, but I had never seen so many diseased, so many starving, so many without limbs. We quickly ran out of small coins to give to them, and my father was in professional paradise.

"Look at that dislocation!" he exclaimed, peering out of the carriage. "I would have to spend years before I saw one of that kind in Leptis, and here I have seen three in the course of an hour! And look – terminal stage elephantiasis! What a place this is for a physician! There is nowhere like Rome!"

My mother and I exchanged a despairing glance, and she opened her travelling box to find some food to give to a dreadfully thin child who was reaching a pitiful little hand up to our carriage. My father was greedily following a clubfoot with his gaze. I sat, feeling miserable and not knowing where to look. It all seemed so sad, so dirty and poor. Where was the glorious Rome we had heard so much about?

As the streets grew narrower and the houses taller, I began to feel terrified simply by the city's sheer size. By now, we would have reached the centre of Leptis Magna. And there were crowds everywhere – the roads were choked with carts and people walking and riders and soldiers. So many people! It was as if they were all being sucked up, swallowed by a huge monstrous mouth.

"How many people live here?" I found myself asking.

"A million, perhaps more," my father replied. "Magnificent, isn't it?"

It *was* magnificent – but it terrified me. It was too big. I felt as if I were drowning.

Carriages were not allowed into the city until nightfall, so when we stopped at a *mansio* to rest, my father left the luggage in the carriage with a slave, and hired some bearers to carry us onwards in litters.

"The Emperor is expecting us," he said. I had never seen him so nervous.

As we went deeper into the city, the noise grew and grew. Six-storey tower blocks – called *insulae* because, like islands, they reared up from the sea of people around them – blocked daylight from the streets. People leaned from their windows to chat with their neighbours, and more than once we had to scoot to avoid a chamber pot being emptied. Arguments and love songs, politicians thundering away, all mingled with the shouts of people selling everything from vegetables to perfume, fish sauce to fine scarves.

"*Caput mundi!*" my father said, as proudly as if he had built Rome himself. "Head of the world, the greatest city there is."

Just as he said that, our bearers stopped. An old man's even older donkey had died in the middle of the road, spilling its baskets of onions everywhere. Helpful Romans, annoyed Romans, pick-pocketing Romans and just plain curious Romans had gathered around. The road was completely blocked.

"Now I see why they demanded an hourly rate," my mother said dryly, peeking through the curtains of the litter. "It will take us a day to reach the palace."

In the end my father hired some more people to clear the way in front of us, and we went slowly onwards. I stared out of the litter, amazed at everything. Everywhere I looked there were more roads, more streets of hammering smiths or busy vegetable markets, more glittering temples heaving out smoke from sacrifices, more steaming bathhouses, more jingling dancers and priests winding their way through the crowds. And the words! So many babbling barbarian voices, so many shrill Roman dialect curses being shrieked, so many arguments and jokes and fights! Even the walls shouted, for wherever I looked there was more rude graffiti than I had ever seen before. All these things were in Leptis Magna too, but there was so much more of them all in Rome. If Leptis was a busy fish pond, Rome was the ocean.

My father was beaming, but my mother sat up as straight and taut as if she were a prisoner. I was terrified, but excited too. Soon we had left the ordinary streets and entered the heart of Rome, where the most important buildings were. Now things were different. There were more soldiers around, and more people in togas, fewer in tunics. Marble glared back the sunlight from arches built to honour great men. The straight lines of the inscriptions made me think of sword cuts, slicing down, then slashing up. Columns towered above the bustling, toga-clad officials. Upon each one, like an eagle watching for prey, perched a statue. Gods and emperors seemed to follow us with their painted eyes, their gilded crowns flashing golden in the sun. And there, among them—

"A girl on a horse!" I exclaimed. I pointed. There was a statue with a girl like me, wearing girls' clothes, astride a horse.

"That's Cloelia," my mother said shortly.

"So girls do ride! Can't I have a horse?"

My mother tutted and my father laughed.

"Cloelia was captured by Rome's enemies in the ancient days of Lars Porsena. She escaped from her captors by stealing a horse and swimming a river, and she took the other captives with her. She was brave, but that was wartime. Horses are for men in Rome, and not just any men – knights and senators."

I was silent. I watched the statue until it was out of sight. The stone girl, voiceless, unnoticed, looked out over the heads of everyone bustling in Rome. Then, as if a river swept me away from her, she was gone.

My father kept up a commentary, pointing out the temples to different gods, the forums built by Julius Caesar and the Senate House.

"Why are there so many soldiers?" I exclaimed, as yet another cohort in jingling armour and scarlet cloaks strode past. "There were fewer in Leptis Magna and we had the Garamantes on our doorstep."

My father and mother exchanged a glance.

"The Emperor is a military man," my father said. "He likes the army."

This still seemed odd to me, but a moment later, I had forgotten about it. For we had reached the enormous entrance to the Palatine Hill, the palace where the emperors of Rome lived. Looking back, I saw the busy forum with dignified senators crossing it, deep in conversation with each other. But when I looked ahead, I saw only soldiers with stony faces and eyes that were about as kind as those of the statues; less, in fact, for the painted eyes of the gods often seemed to smile at me.

Our litter bearers stopped. Soldiers milled around. One centurion flicked open the curtain of our litter with his truncheon and examined us without a smile. I heard questions, orders and instructions. The spears in the hands of the soldiers were like the thorns on a cactus, glinting. I'd once grasped a cactus fruit by mistake and I remembered the pain. I kept my eyes on the spears.

But people were expecting us. The gates opened and we were carried in; then they shut with a crash behind us.

"You were inside the palace? The real, emperor's palace?" Your eyes are wide. "How big was it?"

I think hard. What can you possibly compare it to? I realise for the first time, perhaps, how different your world is to mine. The biggest things you've ever seen are the sky and the sea. The biggest things built by man – well, you can't imagine anything other than our farmhouse. You haven't even seen Londinium.

"Imagine the most magnificent house you've ever been in. It has porticoes, passages, courtyards and gardens. Then imagine that house is surrounded by another house, more courtyards, more pools and gardens, more offices and workrooms. Then surround it with yet another, pathways and passages all branching like a tree. And another. And another. That was how it felt to walk into the palace of the Emperor of Rome."

Now you are really listening. Power is like the sun: you can't ignore it.

You just have to try not to get burned up.

The noise from the city died away as we followed our escort, who was not a soldier this time, but a Greek slave who managed to look down his nose at us despite being a slave. I followed at my mother's heels, trying not to stare as we passed pillars of different coloured marbles, statues covered in silver and gold, murals and mosaics like glittering jewels. Banners and curtains wafted in the breeze, and there was the sound of dancing water from hidden gardens. I caught the occasional glimpse

59

or scent of beautifully dressed people drifting about like nymphs.

Door after door was opened for us and closed behind us. Then, at last, the slave stopped before a door that opened like a picture frame onto a sunny garden, where a woman and two young men sat in golden chairs. Beyond them was only blue sky.

"The imperial family," the slave murmured.

The woman who rose to meet us was Julia Domna, wife of the Emperor. She looked like her pictures, but with one difference – her skin was much darker than it had been painted. Her dark brows almost met in the middle, and her face was severe, with a strongly carved nose and deep-set brown eyes. Her hair was done in a way I had never seen before; it looked almost like a helmet, but you could see it had taken hours of painstaking work to create those regular, regimented braids. It framed her face like a setting frames a jewel. She was not beautiful, but one look at her told me I would never dare disobey her.

Beside her, in golden chairs, sat two men in their twenties. One was older, and very like the Emperor's statues, if the statues had been in a scowling, bad mood. The other, younger one looked more like his mother. I guessed at once that the older one was Bassianus, who was always called Caracalla, and the younger one was Geta.

I remembered the arch of Septimius Severus in Leptis Magna. On that stone, the brothers had been shown grasping hands with their father, tall and straight and in complete agreement. *Concordia*: peace. But the men in front of me were not calm, dignified marble heroes. Caracalla's face was red and puffy and his eyes were sharp and watched every move we made. Geta was pale and fidgety, and he seemed to know when Caracalla's knife-blade eyes were on him.

Even from a distance, I noticed how Caracalla leaned forward as if about to pounce, and how Geta cringed away from him, while trying to pretend he was not afraid. The cats stood like that back at home, when the older kitten was bullying the younger one into a fight he would never win. No, there was no *concordia* here.

"Doctor – I have heard much about your skill," Julia Domna said, sweetly.

My parents walked towards her, responding to the Empress's welcoming smile and her outstretched hand. I hung back, feeling tongue-tied and shy.

A shadow fell across me. I turned and looked up, into the face of the Emperor himself, Septimius Severus.

8.

EAGLES

I recognised Septimius Severus at once from his statues. He was in his sixties, the same age as my father, but he looked older. Pain had scarred his face, and he was leaning on two sticks. When he walked, he hobbled. Still, his arm muscles were strong beneath his purple toga, and he had the face of a fighter.

I do not know what I said or did. Probably nothing, but my expression must have echoed my shock and terror.

"Who do we have here? A nymph unwilling to step into Olympus," said the Emperor. Although I knew he came from Leptis Magna, it was still startling to hear an accent like my own, coming out of the mouth of the Emperor himself. He ushered me forwards into the garden, and the sunlight blazed in my eyes.

"Quintus Camillus, the great physician!" I heard the Emperor exclaim. "Have you finally come to save me from the chalkstones that are crippling my feet?"

The Emperor quickly dropped the Latin and spoke about his health in Punic. He asked my father to take his pulse. What my father diagnosed seemed to please the Emperor. Slaves came to offer us food. One – a boy my age – had a dint under his eye the size and shape of five big knuckles. He stared at the ground as he offered us the golden tray then seemed to vanish with the others into the depths of the gardens. I followed him with my gaze – and spotted the soldiers who guarded the gates, expressionless in scarlet, gold and iron.

Somehow I knew that we were being judged – on our loyalty, our weaknesses, our potential usefulness. I also knew that, like slaves, we could be disposed of if we did not meet the Emperor's needs. Now I understood why my mother said as little as possible and smiled a great deal.

Driven by fear, I edged away from the Emperor and his wife, towards the blue sky. I did not dare look away from the Emperor for fear of being thought disrespectful, until I sensed a drop below me. I looked down behind me, and I realised that the garden ended in a cliff. There was a low wall, and then I looked out over the city of Rome. Red-brick walls and shining marble statues gleamed beneath me. Gilded roofs flashed in the sun, and columns of smoke wavered up from the temples. Below me, steep paths wound down through shady gardens, and even further below, I saw a long, massive loop of bare earth, from which the sound of distant cheers drifted up like the roaring of the sea at the bottom of the steep cliff. It was the chariot-racing stadium, the Circus Maximus, and I had the best view in the city. As I watched, an eagle wheeled slowly, using the tides of the air to lift it. It was close enough that I could see its golden eyes, staring after prey.

Caracalla strolled over to me, and looked over the edge. He spat. It vanished into the distance. He looked at me and smiled, or bared his teeth. I noticed his knuckles were badly bruised.

"No way down but to jump," he said. "Or be thrown."

"Or fly, sir," I said, and regretted it at once.

"Indeed," he said, and gave me a considering gaze. "But only if you are an eagle. Are you an eagle, little girl?"

I glanced back at the wheeling eagle. Eagles were the bird of Jupiter – the bird of the Emperor. They played the air like a skilled general playing the enemy, waiting for the perfect moment to strike their prey, with back-breaking force.

Just as I thought that, the eagle, seeming to read my mind, swooped and vanished into the shadows. I winced, even though I did not see the victim. No, I was certainly no eagle.

"No, sir," I murmured, and wanted to add, but didn't: *I will be lucky if I get out of here without being a roast chicken*.

I turned back to where my father, Julia Domna and the Emperor were conversing. My mother stood a little back, her eyes modestly cast down. I remembered what I had heard of Julia Domna: that she was from a family of immense wealth in distant Syria, priests of Heliogabalus, a god of the sun. She was as tall as the Emperor and I thought they looked at each other with respect.

The Emperor was talking about Britain. I had heard of Britain. It was the last province, a cold island at the end of the Empire. It had some wealth, but it was full of warring, uncivilised tribes with ugly sounding names.

"The Caledonians and the Maetae have overwhelmed the Antonine Wall," the Emperor was saying. "Well, we can't allow this – the borders of the Empire must be secured. The army in Britain want support, and my sons are ready for a campaign, to prove themselves as leaders of men."

He looked sharply at Caracalla as he said this. Caracalla smiled, but it did not reach his eyes.

My father nodded politely.

"But my health is not good, so of course, I thought of you as a personal physician. At least I know you will not poison me, eh, Quintus?" He laughed. My father laughed too, although I was not sure how funny anyone found it.

"I can assure you—" my father began, but the Emperor waved him silent.

"Don't assure me, Quintus, I despise broken promises." The Emperor laughed again, but this time no one else did. "Simply use your genius to keep me in good health, and you will find it worth your while. We were boys together. You have no son. You have a daughter whom I have no objection to settling well – even if a senator's son is a high prize for a doctor's daughter."

I froze as all attention turned to me.

"And so we will be departing as soon as the gods allow," the Emperor went on. "You may first conclude the marriage. I have arranged for her and Publius to meet at his house. One should always meet before one is married."

"Departing?" my father said.

"For Britain. As my personal physician, I will need you by my side throughout the campaign against the Caledonians."

I had always admired my father. I admired his wisdom, his clever mind and surgeon's fingers. Sometimes his cures seemed almost magical. But I never admired him more than at that moment, when he pulled hope out of his worst disappointment. He had finally, after years of scheming and string-pulling, arrived at the one place in the world that he wanted to be – Rome. When the Emperor said he was to go at once to Britain his expression broke, like a reflection in a still pool when a stone is thrown into it. But he only lost control for a second. Then he pulled himself together, drew himself up tall and behaved as if nothing could please him more than to go to the freezing, bleak barbarian land that made Leptis Magna look as magnificent as Rome.

"I shall be honoured to serve my emperor, even to the very ends of the Empire," he said, and bowed.

"We are glad to hear it, are we not?" The Emperor glanced at his sons.

"Very glad," Geta said.

Caracalla just smiled. However, as we prepared to leave the garden, he said lazily: "Hey, doctor – what would you advise for this little bruise of mine?"

He raised his clenched fist up to my father's face, so fast that my father flinched back. It was the fist with the bruised knuckles I had noticed before.

My father recovered quickly. Putting on his professional manner in a way that terrified me but also made me proud, he coolly took Caracalla's hand and turned it back and forth, observing it as if it were no more than anyone else's hand. There was a short silence.

"I advise, my lord, that you stop hitting your slaves," my father said quietly, releasing Caracalla's hand. "All the philosophers are against mindless violence."

There was a horrifying pause in which I felt as if my entire stomach had plummeted to the Circus Maximus below and been trampled on by maddened horses. Then the Emperor burst out into a roar of approving laughter.

"Very good, Quintus, very good!" he said, slapping my father on the back. "Exactly what I always tell him. But he never listens to me."

Caracalla smiled thinly, and Geta sniggered, and Julia Domna called for some slaves to take us to our rooms so we could rest. I walked away, feeling Caracalla watching us the whole way.

As soon as we were alone in our apartments, my father sat down by the window and stared out at the palace gardens.

"A good philosopher must treat good news and bad news exactly the same," he said. I knew he wanted to be cheerful for us, but his voice sounded empty and my heart ached for him. "What a blessing philosophy is."

We waited, not daring to say anything in case we upset him even more. After a few long moments, he pulled himself upright and gave us a smile.

"Britain won't be for long," he said firmly. "And as we will be on a battlefield, I may even get a dead barbarian to dissect – think of that! The law against dissecting humans has held medicine back for so long."

"Cutting up a dead person, against all the gods – to think I should live to see the day!" As if my father putting a brave face on it had given her a licence to show her feelings again, my mother threw her veil over her face and rocked back and forth.

"Well, dear, you won't see it. It will be best if you remain in Rome to support Camilla in her new marriage," my father replied. "You will need to see no dead barbarians at all."

So, I was going to be married. In the next few weeks, if I understood rightly. I realised I was shaking. I picked up a shawl and wrapped it tightly around me so that no one would see how frightened I was. I was absolutely terrified. I clutched the amulet Nurse had given me. I wished she were there; I would have forgiven her everything.

9.

THE GHOST OF A MARRIAGE

I was to meet Publius the very next day, at his family's house. Before we left, my mother had the slaves spend hours on my hair and arranging my dress. They were palace slaves, so they had high standards. Ropes of amber and gold were wrapped around my throat. Whitening lead make-up was rubbed over my face, and ochre was daubed on my lips and cheeks to make them look red. My hair was waved like the Empress's, which meant tucking wads of hair that used to belong to some unfortunate slave girl under my own hair to give it volume. By the end of it my neck was stiff with being held upright and my eyes ached from looking in the mirror. I no longer even looked like myself.

Then my father came in in a rage and made me wash it all off.

"Absolute nonsense," he told my mother. "That white lead that rich women smear on their faces is bad for the health. It can poison, even as far as death if it is used too much. That was written in the *Alexipharmaca* of Nicander, the great Greek physician. No daughter of mine is using it."

"But everyone uses it," my mother protested. "Even the Empress!"

"Not my daughter," my father repeated firmly. "It's bad for the health."

My mother shrugged. "Oh well," she said with a sigh, "perhaps it is for the best. It may be fashionable, but it made you look too grown-up. He is marrying a girl, after all, not an adult woman on her second husband."

So, in the end, I went to meet Publius wearing a fashionable hairstyle, gold earrings and necklace, perfume, but no make-up. I didn't care. I felt sick with nerves and I just wanted to get the meeting over with.

The house itself was a villa in the heart of the city's finest district. Slaves unbarred the door for us and we went in over the mosaic floor, into the wide, pleasant courtyard filled with the scent of blossom and grapes dangling overhead. Publius's mother, a plump, giggly woman with house keys jingling at her waist, came out to meet us, and embraced my mother – the two had been friends before I was born.

"You have such a cute accent!" she exclaimed, pinching my cheeks in a way I hated. "Just like the Emperor himself, may he live forever! I couldn't understand a word the man was saying when I first met him. I suppose everyone sounds like that in the provinces."

I hardly heard her. I was looking around trying to guess which of the young men I saw might be Publius. His mother led me over to him. I recognised his long-lashed eyes and his shy expression. The knobbly elbows were gone, however, and I wished Livia were there, because I could have told her: he *was* handsome.

"Mother!" You look at me, shocked. I have to laugh.

"What? There are other handsome men in the world than your father, you know," I tease. "Anyway, he wasn't just handsome. He was. . ." I search for the right word. Gentle, modest. . . and yet those weren't the things that made me feel at ease with him. "Kind."

Our mothers sat a polite distance away from us, while Publius and I walked awkwardly together around the large pool in the courtyard. He was twenty, slim and quiet with dark curly hair, and not much suited to the senatorial toga he wore. I expected the purple stripe to be on fat, old men with bald heads and wrinkles. He seemed rather embarrassed by his, instead of honoured.

"I don't usually wear this at home," he told me in a low voice. "After all, it's my father who is the senator – not me."

I said very little at first, suddenly feeling too shy and awkward to talk. It was not as if I had never met any men before. I was used to my father's friends, who enjoyed loud philosophical discussions over plenty of wine and a good meal, but that was different; I wasn't expected to marry *them*. Suddenly I felt I had to prove I would be a good wife. Publius seemed to notice that I was tongue-tied, and kindly asked me questions I could answer, about my life in Leptis Magna, and about my reading.

This was something I could be confident about.

"I have read all of Virgil, and Cicero, and the Greek philosophers, and the writings of Marcus Aurelius... but my favourite is the *Aeneid*."

"It is a wonderful story," he said. "It has everything – burning cities, shipwreck, adventure, love..." He broke off, blushing. He was clearly as embarrassed as I was about being reminded of the reason we were here. I wished we could just have a conversation without the ghost of marriage hanging over us the whole time.

"I am glad you are educated," he said finally. "So many girls are not, and it makes them very dull to talk to. It seems, to me anyway—" he glanced shyly at me

"—that we will get along together very well, if we can talk about the same things."

After our visit, when my mother leaned across to me in the carriage and asked, "Well?" – looking into my face as demandingly as a tax collector – it really was not that hard to make myself smile and nod: *I like him.*

I saw Publius almost every day after that. He never again wore the senatorial toga; he wore a plain toga over a simple tunic. We talked about my favourite places in Leptis Magna, and we discussed philosophy and literature.

Once, Caracalla came with us.

I was never sure exactly why he came. I suspected that it was to inspect Publius, to see if he was a threat. But Publius was so obviously gentle and unassuming that Caracalla, after a few questions that were as pointed and loaded as ballista missiles, got up abruptly, snatched a peach from the silver fruit bowl and strode off, ignoring both the hostess and Publius. His visit gave me a new insight into Publius, however, because that was the only time I ever heard him sound angry.

"I dislike that man," he said, although his voice sounded as if he had said *hate* instead of *dislike*.

"Me too," I replied at once, without thinking whether this was a wise thing to say, or a wife-like thing to say. I met his eyes and I saw Publius meant it.

"He is cruel," Publius went on, his fists clenching. "He has his slaves whipped for the slightest offence, and I have heard tales—" He stopped, scowling to himself. "I shall not repeat them." Then he burst out: "I don't believe we should have slaves at all. People are not for owning. If we were to free all ours, when we are married, what would you say?"

I was taken aback. We had always had slaves. I really didn't know what we would do without them. Who would do the washing, I wondered, and the cooking, and the cleaning? And what on earth would Publius's father – a grand old man of a senator – say? It seemed completely unrealistic to me. But. . .

"I would say it was a good idea," I said, and smiled at him.

He looked into my face, as if trying to judge how much he could trust me. What he saw seemed to please him. He smiled.

"You must miss Leptis Magna," he said. He hesitated. "Once we are married, we could travel there perhaps. For a visit."

My eyes filled with tears. I hadn't realised how nervous I had been feeling, or how much depended on him being kind. I knew I was lucky in the man I was betrothed to.

But I also realised that I needed to be lucky. What happened in my life did not depend on me, but on the whim of the Emperor and the goodwill of the man I was told to marry. I felt glad and happy that Publius was going to be a good husband, but a shadow was cast over it by the knowledge that it was just luck. At any moment, a wave might come and knock my sandcastle life to pieces.

As I talked to Publius over the next few days, I learned more about Roman politics. When I asked whether his father and the Emperor were friends, Publius shook his head.

"The Emperor and the senate are not friends. Too many senators had their noses put out of joint by a provincial general taking control after they had spent years working to gain power," he added. "That is why the Emperor is encouraging us two to marry. He wants to make some alliances among his friends and the senate."

"But doesn't the Emperor rule by the will of the senate?"

"Not this emperor. No, he rules by the will of the army. No one dares rebel, not when all the men with swords are loyal to him. If you cross him. . ." He made a gesture of slitting a throat with his hand.

"Like Plautianus," I said, remembering.

"Yes, that was a scandal. The man was powerful, but Caracalla hated being married off to his daughter. Poor little Plautilla. She was sent off to the ends of the earth, and her father was dead soon after. Caracalla has his own plans and the Emperor won't be able to hold him back for long." He sounded bitter. "This is Rome, full of murderers, liars and thieves. One day they will all be called to answer to God."

That last word rang oddly in my ears, and I began to suspect something. As it turned out, I was right to be suspicious.

10.

GODLESS

A few days later, my mother was unwell and unable to travel to Publius's house. The Empress herself said she would act as chaperone for me. She brought her secretary with her, and sat dictating letters to him as Publius and I strolled in the gardens.

At the end of the gardens was a grotto, overhung with cool plants and with the trickle of water. As we reached it, Publius turned to me, a serious look on his face.

"I have something for you," he said under his breath. And then, to my surprise, "Don't tell your mother."

I looked at the flash of gold in his outstretched hand. It was a golden seal ring. It did not show a god, or the Emperor's head. Instead, cut into the amber stone was the Greek letter *chi* crossed with the letter *rho*. I knew as soon as I saw it that this piece of jewellery could put me in danger.

"You're a Christian," I breathed.

He nodded.

I'd heard plenty of stories about Christians. They were a Jewish sect, but their ideas had spread to others too. They were traitors to the Empire, traitors to the gods. They didn't pray in the natural way, proudly in public to the holy gods of Rome, but in private, like thieves. And worse stories, too.

"Do you eat human flesh?" I blurted out.

"Of course not!" He looked shocked. "Is that what they say about us?"

It was one of the things they said about them. I had never quite believed it, and looking at Publius, I was sure he did not. But even so, Christians were not just like worshippers of Mithras or Heliogabalus. They refused to worship the gods at *all*. My father called Christians *átheos*, which meant *godless* in Greek. He usually treated all sects and religions equally, but the Christians: those he did not like. I did not know why, but I guessed it was because they did not worship the gods. I understood, because not worshipping the gods was dangerous. It could only lead to destruction, when the gods grew angry at being disrespected and sent down some terrible force. Cities were destroyed by the Earth-shaker

Neptune, Jupiter struck with lightning – all these things killed not just Christians but everyone else, too.

Publius was looking at the amulet on my wrist, the one my nurse had given me. I had seen him looking at it before, and now I had a sinking feeling. Christians did not like what they called idols.

"What is that?"

My other hand closed protectively over it.

"My nurse gave it to me. It's a good-luck charm."

"If we are to marry," he said, "you must, like me, abandon false gods and idols."

I clutched my amulet. I didn't know what to say. I had no desire to give up my religion. To abandon Diana, Isis, Asclepius, Hygeia and Salus? To throw away my Lares and Penates? I had not realised how important they were to me, until now.

"I can't do that!"

"I cannot marry a woman who does not share my faith." He sounded sad. "And I'd like to marry you."

I remained silent. I wanted to marry him too. But not if it meant giving up everything that meant most to me.

"Do you truly believe there can be any power in this thing?" He caught my wrist gently. "Don't be afraid. If I throw it in the water, do you think that any of your gods will strike me down?"

I realised I did believe that, because terror hit me like a wave. I liked Publius. I didn't want him to be destroyed by the furious gods. And I was terrified of losing the amulet, the only thing I had left of Nurse and her love for me, and home itself.

"Let go!" I pulled away from him, turned and went towards the Empress. I heard his footsteps behind me and broke into a run in a blind panic.

The Empress rose to meet me and I ran, sobbing, full tilt into her. It was like running into a steel bar. She grabbed my shoulders and gave me a quick, sharp shake that knocked the tears out of me.

"What has happened?" she asked, seeing my face.

"I want to go home," I managed to say.

She tutted.

"Young men," she said with annoyance. She cast a cold look at Publius, who looked terrified. She nodded to the secretary who had come up behind us. "Call the carriage."

I was shaking, wondering what I could say to explain matters. To be a Christian was a shameful thing for the son of a senator. If I could hide the ring, I thought, then perhaps I could make up some story. But she was not the Empress for nothing. As soon as we sat in the carriage she reached out for my hand that was grasping the ring.

"Dear, what's that?" she asked. "Let me see your treasure."

I could not refuse. I handed her the ring. She turned it over and over with some curiosity.

"Are you a Christian?" she said.

I shook my head hard.

"It was a... gift from someone," I muttered, blushing. Then, my tongue lying faster than I knew it could: "I wanted to show Publius. So that there would be no secrets in our marriage."

"Ah, a gift from some old boyfriend. I see now. But you worship the gods too, I see by this amulet."

I hastily assured her that my devotion to the gods and ancestors of Rome was total. She did not seem overly concerned by the ring, however. Having the amulet – something normal – on me as well as the ring, seemed to reassure her that I was no Christian. If Publius had been asked before the courts if he was a Christian he would not have been able to deny it, and then he would have been executed.

"Have you heard of Apollonius of Tyana?" she said, handing the ring back to me. "Now he is the one you should be following, not Jesus. He is a true mystic, not a charlatan. He did everything that Jesus claimed to have done, but there are better witnesses to his miracles."

"I would be happy to read more of him," I said, eager to please her.

"Good, then I will find some writings for you. There is nothing wrong with seeking for truth in many different places. Only don't forget: gods are important not because they tell us what to do, but because they tell us who we are." She handed the ring back to me. "And this?" She pointed to the amulet.

"My old nurse gave it to me. She was from the tribe of the Garamantes."

"The desert people," Julia Domna said. "Did she come with you to Rome?"

"I think she died of grief rather than leave her home," I said quietly.

It was the first time I had ever admitted my thoughts, even to myself. You hide things from yourself because they are too painful to see. Nurse had been the only mother I had really known, closer than my own mother. But she was enslaved. She had become my wet nurse because she had breasts full of milk, for a baby who was not me. Who did she secretly think of when she fed me? Was there a small grave that she did not want to leave behind her? Every so often, in Leptis Magna as well as in other cities, the bodies of those too old and weak and poor to live were pulled from the sea. An old woman, penniless and hunted by the law, could only disappear into death.

Julia Domna looked at me, her head on one side. I wondered what *she* hid from herself. I thought of Caracalla and Geta, twitching their tails and muttering curses like rival tomcats.

"A brave woman then," she said. "Who died with honour despite being a slave."

She must have made up her mind on that carriage ride, because when we stepped out at the palace, she announced it as a fact.

"Your daughter is too young to marry," she said to my mother. "She can come to Britain with us, and when we return to Rome I will arrange a husband for her. She can do better than Publius."

My mother opened her mouth, then closed it again. There was nothing she could say. It was not a question, it was a statement by the most powerful woman in the world.

"You are favoured," she said to me when we were alone. "The Empress herself takes an interest in you."

Yes, I thought, *as the eagle takes an interest in the chicken!*

I told my father the truth about what had happened.

"You did the right thing," he said with a frown. "I am disappointed in Publius."

"You won't tell anyone, will you?" I begged him. "They would kill him – and Christians don't eat human flesh. He said they don't, and I believe him!"

He smiled sadly. "No, they don't eat human flesh. But they are required to believe through faith, not through the arguments of philosophy. And that is a dangerous path, which leads far from Rome."

That night, I went to my apartments and removed my rich clothes and my jewels. I undid my tight, uncomfortable hairstyle. Outside my window, I could see one of the many pools filled with fish, flicking their tails, swimming back and forth, without ever being able to find a way out of their prison. Water and light rippled on white marble.

When I had changed into simpler clothes, I sat down at the window. In the light of the setting sun, I took off Nurse's amulet. I had only ever taken it off to change the string before. The prayer itself was contained inside a hollow reed, sealed with red wax.

I dug my nail into the wax. The reed cracked open. There was no going back now, although my chest felt tight and painful. I broke open the reed and a thin scrap of papyrus came curling out. There was faded writing on it. I hadn't been sure I would understand it, for the priests of Isis used strange symbols sometimes, but I was lucky: this prayer was written in Greek. I read it carefully.

It was what Nurse had said it was – a prayer to keep a baby safe from harm. But it was not a prayer for me.

It was not my name written on the papyrus. It was a stranger's.

Now I knew the truth. It had never been meant for me at all. I was second-best. All my life, I had been wearing a good-luck charm that Nurse had bought not for me but for her own baby, who had died just before I was born. The dead child had left me an inheritance of her mother's milk – and this amulet.

We must treat bad news and good news exactly the same, I said to myself silently. I looked up and out of the window at the sun setting over the Palatine Hill. Tears pricked behind my eyes, but I thought of all the Stoic philosophers I had ever read. What would Marcus Aurelius say? *After all, we are all going to die soon, so what is the sense of weeping?* It helped, in that it made everything seem so miserable that I couldn't decide what to cry about first, so in the end I didn't cry at all. Instead, I watched blankly through the window as a slave came out of the shadows, carrying a long net, which he dipped unhurriedly into the gilded water to snare a fish for the Emperor's dinner.

11.

FIGS IN WINTER

The wind rustles the long grass and a distant lonely bird calls. It's cold and quiet and so, so far from Rome.

I've talked myself into the past, and it seems strange to me to think that Britain has been my home for twenty years and more now. People I love have been born here; people I love have died here. Is that what makes a place a home? Or will home always be the place I grew up in, the city I will never go back to – Leptis Magna?

I could do it. If I really wanted to, I could go back. Just a few weeks and I would be standing on the quay at Leptis Magna, the sun warming my body through to the bone. I would be looking up at the lighthouse's trail of smoke, listening to the old familiar accents of the sailors and traders working the harbour, mingling with the snarl of caged beasts on their way to Rome. And the smells! Bread doesn't smell the same here as it does at home, and fish sauce doesn't taste the same.

"Well?" you say behind me. "What happened next, Ma?"

And I know I can't leave. Because I know that as I stood looking up at the lighthouse, I would be missing, to the very bone, everything about Britain. I would miss the cool rain in the air, the soft change of the light. I would miss your laughter as you play outside, and your father grumbling to himself as he struggles with some leaky window frame or warped wheel rim he's trying to fix. He's always trying to make this place better, for me and for you. When I came here, it was built of wood. He turned it into stone for me. He even laid a mosaic floor, so I could close my eyes and pretend I was barefoot at home. Not that it worked. Mosaics here are always cold and damp.

"Next," I say, swallowing down my sadness. "Next, we set out for Britain. We travelled over the sea to Spain, then up through Gaul. It was a long way. The Emperor was in such pain that he could not travel in a carriage; he had to be carried in a litter the whole way. It was a long, dusty journey and when we got to the coast, and we could tell ourselves we saw the shores of Britain ahead of us, we were so happy because we thought that it was nearly the end of our journey. The Classis Britannica was there, the fleet that ferried soldiers over the short gap of sea to Britain, and we thought we couldn't be safer."

"But then there was the storm," you say.

"Yes, then there was the storm." Even now it is hard to think of it without feeling sick.

"When my grandmother drowned."

"Yes. When we got to Britain, we were not a family any more – we were like an arch when one stone falls down and the rest tumble after it."

"Was there no grave for my grandmother?" you ask. You look serious – you know how important it is to be remembered.

"We put up a memorial. For all I know it is still there – in the port, at Londinium."

London was larger than I expected, more Roman than I expected. We stood on the deck and watched as the long stone walls slid into view. The eagle standards, symbol of the Empire, flew above everything. The sludgy river carried us past banks where wooden houses and fishing boats huddled. Children with strange, reddened skins ran and played on the bank, shouting to each other in the odd, bird-like languages of British tribes. But as we docked we heard the sound of Latin, mixed with Punic and Gaulish and other, stranger languages. It was not so different from Leptis Magna, after all. It was a Roman city, with all the things a Roman city should have. There was a lighthouse and a temple to Jupiter, and further in we could see the forum and the basilica. Of course, it was

91

not Rome. It was more built of wood than of stone, but you felt you were in the Empire. It was only the heavy grey cloud above and the sense that there was damp everywhere, unseen, in the air, that troubled me. My woollen cloak already felt water-logged. The cloud pressed down on my spirits. Where was the sun?

"There is the Emperor's ship," my father said, pointing to the great mast that towered over all the other ships.

The imperial family were nowhere in sight, but I could tell by the glint on gilded eagle standards where they must be. The soldiers were thickest there, like a moving forest of iron.

The sailors threw down the gangplank. I tugged my woollen cloak tighter around me. I turned to look for my mother and just like the sun, she wasn't there. Despite the lurch in my stomach, I walked down the gangplank with my father and, just like that, we were in Britain. I was not expecting to have to get used to being on land again. My legs wobbled and I almost fell. My father caught me. I could see in his face he was worried about me.

"We will get a litter for you," he told me, "and a maid." He glanced around, trying like me, to make sense of where we were. Although the huge, busy, bustling port was reassuringly Roman, we saw a host of exotic tribesmen, with pale skins and long blond or reddish hair, striding here and there. *Barbarians!* I thought, fascinated. Some of them had blue eyes, which I found disturbing – no eye should be so pale.

The captain of our ship was speaking to a centurion with a narrow, bronzed face and one eye missing, puckered into a scar. The centurion glanced towards us now and then as they spoke. Then he walked over to us, removed his helmet and nodded to my father.

"*Ave!* I am Marcus Caecilius Naso, one of the Emperor's personal guards. I have been sent by the Emperor to act as your escort. No doubt you will wish to rest after your long journey."

"Thanks to the Emperor," my father replied gratefully. "Please show us somewhere my daughter can rest. I must replenish the stores of medicines I lost in the wreck – and I must also sacrifice to the gods in memory of my poor wife."

"Of course," Marcus said, looking sympathetic. "Follow me."

As we walked, Marcus asked: "Do you have any questions?" It was directed at my father, but also at me, in a polite sort of way.

I looked around us at the bustling port. *I should have questions,* I thought. *I should have all kinds of intelligent, insightful questions. I should be interested in the barbarian ways, in the peoples of Britain and the campaign of the Emperor.* My father was already asking about where he could get bitumen and foxgloves and other ingredients for his medicine chest. But I couldn't think of any questions, except one, which I knew was probably going to make me sound stupid. I pulled my woollen cloak closer around my shoulders and asked it anyway, as soon as there was a space in their conversation.

"When will it be summer?"

My father and Marcus gaped at me.

"This *is* summer," said Marcus.

Then they both burst out laughing. I was right. It had made me sound stupid, and my heart sank at the thought that the sun was never coming back. *This might be summer for Britain,* I thought, *but it was winter for me.* Without the sun it could never be anything but winter. But I laughed along with them anyway, because it was good to see my father smiling, even if it was only out of surprise, for the first time since we lost my mother.

We went to a stonemason who worked in a street by the river. He sold tombstones that were already carved with the right portraits: for women, for men and for children. I found myself staring at one that was carved with a whole family group: mother, father and two children. The stonemason followed my gaze.

"Cheaper than having one each," he explained cheerfully. "You buy it for the first of you to go, and pop the others under the same stone when it's their time."

The stone was local stuff and my father worried about it. Was British stone good enough for my mother? Would it last?

"Don't worry about it," the stonemason told him. "Fifty years I've been doing this work. I've never had a memorial fall down yet. This limestone will outlast the Empire!" And he gave it a hefty blow with his dusty hand, as if to prove it.

We took his word for it. We had to, after all. We bought a ready-made tombstone for a woman, and my father dictated a short inscription that the stonemason's apprentice chiselled onto it.

DIS MANIBUS: TO THE SPIRITS OF THE DEPARTED.

MARCIA NUMIDIA, WHO LIVED 39 YEARS, SEVEN

MONTHS AND SIX DAYS. NEPTUNE TOOK HER.

SHE WAS A GOOD WIFE AND A GOOD MOTHER.

It didn't seem enough to me, but what else was there to say? The stonemason charged for each letter. I didn't like the fact that it could be any woman on the stone, but again, we had no choice. Our orders were to accompany the Emperor to Eboracum the very next day. There was no time to get the perfect memorial stone. Nothing was happening the way I had expected it to.

The stone was set up just outside the city walls, and my father poured a libation in front of it and we said a prayer.

I closed my eyes and prayed before the memorial in the cold wind of a strange land that still felt unsteady beneath my feet. *Please, gods, be kind to her spirit.*

"Camilla! Camilla!"

Mother was calling me, her voice high and urgent. She stood by a spring, which gushed water over bare, cold, grassy British hills. But the water was frozen and there was ice on the rocks.

"Ma!"

She stretched out her arms to me, and I ran towards her. But as soon as I threw my arms around her, she vanished like smoke or mist. I fell forwards – and woke with a start.

The light was all wrong; dreary and damp. Was I

still dreaming? I rolled upright from the bed, and the hollow, sick feeling in my stomach was there before I realised why it was there: it was a dream – my mother was dead. I was in a room in the *mansio*, the inn of the port where all the weary travellers first went to collapse when they landed from the river. My father had told me to rest while he went out to the market to get medicines.

And yet I still ran downstairs in case somehow, somehow. . . because dreams come from the gods, after all.

I came out into the courtyard, blinking and confused. By the looks of things it was late in the day, but although the sun was hidden behind thick veils of clouds the light still stayed around, like a guest that wouldn't leave. I noticed I was not the only one who was slinking around, glancing at the heavy grey sky mistrustfully as if, like the Gauls, they feared it would one day fall on their heads. I was expecting everything to be different, but the voices and the houses and the shops around me were the same, like Rome. What *was* different were the things I wasn't expecting to change. The light. And my mother. She was not there, though her voice had sounded so real.

I still couldn't quite believe she was really gone. Already the storm felt like a bad dream. I kept expecting her to come around the corner, just a little delayed, breathless, anxious and saying: "Now you are soon to be married. . ." But she was not there.

Instead, I spotted Marcus striding across the courtyard and ran after him.

"Where is my father?" I said in a voice that was practically a panicked shriek.

He looked at me startled. At once, I felt embarrassed for throwing myself in his path like this. He already had plenty of work to do, after all – how could he also be expected to look after a lost, confused girl?

"With the Emperor, long may he live. We are setting out today for Eboracum."

I nodded, though I had no idea where or what Eboracum was. As long as I was with my father, I was sure everything would be all right.

"What should I do?" I asked, hoping to sound more sensible.

"I should gather your possessions together and make ready to leave, miss." He was looking over my shoulder. A moment later, he was gone, striding away to handle another emergency or crisis.

I rushed back to my room. My things were few and easily put in their box. Should I pack my father's things? I wondered. Slaves had always done things like this for us. I had never expected to wash up in Britain like flotsam. I felt suddenly that I wanted to do it myself. At least then I would have some control over what happened.

My father's razor, his togas and books, all went into the box. I hesitated over his wax writing tablet: should I touch that? Was it private? I put it in, trying not to look at it in case there was some writing showing on the wax. Then I closed up his medicine box and sat on his trunk, my heart beating hard. *He will come back for his things,* I thought. He wouldn't be able to leave me behind.

A few moments later, my father raced in. He stopped and stared at me in confusion.

"I am ready," I told him.

"So I see!" He shook his head. "Very well, go to the Empress. She has kindly said you may travel in her carriage."

I was not sure how I felt about that, but I did as I was told. The Empress had never been anything but kind to me, but she was also terrifying. The most powerful woman in the world could not avoid being terrifying, but Julia Domna was more than just the Emperor's wife. She gave the impression that she could have run the Empire quite well on her own.

But when I timidly joined the imperial group, Julia Domna smiled indulgently at me. She did not look as if she had been on a long sea voyage. Her stola was as perfectly draped as that of a statue's, and not a hair was out of place.

"My poor child, you have lost your mother. Now I will be a mother to you," she announced. There was sympathetic murmuring from some of her attendants, curious and resentful glances from others. All were much older than me, except for a couple of the slave girls who were really just there to pour perfume and scatter rose petals at the right moment. Feeling awkward, I bowed my head and murmured something grateful. As I stepped into the carriage, the air was heavy with the perfume of her hair, arranged like a gladiator's helmet.

With a shout and a crack of the whip, the heavy carriage rattled and rolled into movement. We were leaving London. We went through the streets and out through the great gates, turning onto the road that led north. From now on, every mile took us further from safety, deeper into the land of barbarians.

Julia Domna opened a small wooden box and offered it to me. I could not believe what I saw inside, nestling in the straw.

"Fresh figs!" I exclaimed. My father's words – *let us not wish for figs in winter* – came back to me. If you were an empress, it seemed, you could wish for anything you liked. You could carry summer with you in a box.

"A taste of home," Julia Domna said with a smile.

The fig was not as sweet as it would have tasted in Leptis Magna. In fact, I thought it tasted salty, like seawater. The memory of the shipwreck rushed back to me and I had to force myself to swallow the fruit. A moment of panic gripped me as I thought: *We're leaving my mother behind.*

I turned to the window to try to find one last glimpse of the river. Above Londinium, the clouds were a deep grey like an iron sword, and a rainbow hung in the air.

"Beautiful," I whispered. And yet, I missed the sun so much.

I must have looked about to leap from the carriage because Julia Domna leaned forward and gripped my wrist. Her hand was gentle, but powerful. She looked into my eyes, serene and mysterious as one of the Fates.

"Poor child," she said again. But this time it sounded like a warning.

12.

AMONG THE BARBARIANS

We travelled up to Eboracum on the bad, British roads. They weren't paved like the ones everywhere else. Instead they were covered in a layer of gravel, which flung chips and dust up and stung the horses' legs. But a Roman road is never a dull place, and there was plenty to break up the boredom and the discomfort, though sometimes I felt so jolted that I thought my head would shake loose from my body and tumble to the ground like a stone.

There were carts full of clucking chickens and barrels of wine all the way from Lugdunum in Gaul; there were oxen hauling timber and grit, driven by sweating, swearing men up the hills. There were Northern barbarians with hair the colour of flame. There were pedlars and beggars and every so often, a speedy rider carrying official business, their horses' hooves thundering up the dust. There were sheep and pigs and slaves and goats on their way to market.

The Emperor was carried in a litter all the way. I barely saw it, for it was surrounded at all times by the Praetorian Guard, his personal guard: a wall of scarlet and gold and steel. Not all of these were Roman. Some were barbarians. My father said that he had a much bigger guard than previous emperors had had.

"The Emperor doesn't care where men come from as long as they are good soldiers," Marcus told us. "The army love him. He has made us rich and given us freedom and honours. I can marry my wife now, and not fear leaving her penniless when I die."

Of course he had to say that, but it seemed true – the Emperor was greeted with great cheers whenever we entered an army town or garrison. And Britain seemed full of army towns and garrisons, as we went further and further north. A grey, bleak land, I thought, full of hard stones and hard faces. But wherever the Emperor stopped, he made things appear. As if he were a god, from whose feet – gouty and painful as they were – gold flowed and flowers blossomed. Timber buildings were torn down and new stone ones leaped up, soldiers building them faster and in a more organised way than I had ever seen building happen before. New temples were built to honour the Emperor, and palaces were created almost overnight for him to rest in.

We stopped at Lindum first. The land all around was flat and marshy, and boats seemed to move across the fields by magic.

"It's the canals," Marcus said with clear pride. "We dug them out and connected the rivers, and drained the land. Now everything that was useless, fever-ridden marsh is as good as a road. Better!"

Wherever we stopped, my father drew a small crowd of suffering, hopeful locals who had heard that a doctor travelled with the Emperor. Just as in Leptis Magna, he did not turn anyone away, day or night. He took their pulses and drew their blood and prescribed medicine for them if their four humours – blood, yellow bile, black bile and phlegm – were out of balance.

"The more patients you treat, the more you learn about how the human body works," he told me.

Ever since we left Rome, he had been treating the Emperor's chalkstones with a method he had learned from the great doctor, Galen: mix rancid cheese with cooked, pickled pig's meat, and apply to the feet as a plaster. I had the job of pounding up the cheese and the meat in a mortar and pestle.

"There is no one I trust as much as you," he told me.

The mixture smelt eye-wateringly bad, but the

Emperor dutifully reclined every evening with his feet up and the stinking mixture lavishly smeared all over them.

I found myself mixing up and dispensing medicines, and I actually found it interesting. After a while, a few people started coming to me for help – the humblest ones, like the slaves, who would not dare go to my father. I was especially flattered when Marcus, who had been watching us closely and curiously, one day shyly showed me an infected fingernail and asked what I suggested for it. Not that I was sure what to suggest. It seemed to me that my father could perform wonders with surgery, but the medicines we gave out were much less reliable. Certainly, the cheese-and-ham treatment did not seem to be working for the Emperor. His chalkstones were as bad as ever.

I also began fetching and carrying for Julia Domna. She had discovered somehow that I was educated, and knew how to read and write Greek and Latin, and so I found myself in charge of her social correspondence.

"Call my maids to undress me," the Empress would tell me with a yawn, and then, as the women removed the sandals from her feet and bathed them in rose water, she dictated her letters to me. The letters were usually notes to the wives of the most important men in the area, summoning them to meet her. Sometimes though, they were written to people in Rome, or in Syria, and seemed to hide mysteries under polite words. I realised I was useful to her because I was educated, obedient and completely ignorant of politics. I was a writing machine: too far beneath contempt to pose any kind of danger to them. I hoped – as I handed the sealed notes to the messenger – that they would continue to see me that way.

"Try to swim silently, little fish," my father murmured to me. "It's a big pond – hide yourself well."

It was by being so close to the Empress that I came to realise that Caracalla and Geta fought endlessly. They bickered under their breath as soon as they saw each other – anything could set it off, from one stepping through a door before the other, to a quarrel over the merits of some charioteer back in Rome. As soon as the doors to whatever palace we had stolen for the night had closed behind them, the bickering broke out into real, bitter arguments. When I first saw them snarling and shouting at each other, I was terrified. I thought the Emperor would have them executed. But he just looked at them with weary contempt, and I realised that this must have been going on for a very long time. It was almost, I thought, as if they knew that all their father wanted was for them to get along, and that this was the one thing they could withhold from him. After all, they were his heirs. What could he do to punish them without putting himself in danger?

Everywhere we went, we stood out for more reasons than simply being the Emperor's household. We were Libyans, Africans – our accent, our curly hair and our skin colouring all showed it. Some of the barbarians we passed on the road gaped at us as if we were gods. That was a surprise.

In Rome, the great aristocratic Roman families, the senators, were deeply proud of their heritage that went all the way back to the earliest days of the city of Rome. They looked down on people from the provinces – anywhere in the Empire that wasn't Rome itself. People from senatorial families, like Publius' mother, had always privately mocked the Emperor's Libyan accent, even if they didn't dare to in public. Septimius Severus might spread gold and death around like a god, but to the senators, he would still be a nobody from the provinces, an outsider. They feared him, but they did not respect him. Things were different in Britain. No one looked down on us for being from the provinces, because everyone here was just as provincial as we were. It was rare, in Britain, to find anyone who spoke with a pure Roman accent the way that Publius's family did.

It was clear to see, even with the discomfort of travel and the pain his feet gave him, that the Emperor was happier here than he had been in Rome. After all, this was what he was used to – being away from Rome, on campaign with the army. This was how he had made himself emperor. He wanted Caracalla and Geta to enjoy this life, too. But wherever we stopped, the brothers would skulk off sooner or later to find the nearest bear baiting or boxing match or gladiator competition. If it was violent, Caracalla enjoyed it, and Geta just seemed to like throwing money around, especially in company with soldiers. Meanwhile, a light burned till late at night in the imperial apartments, as the Emperor and Empress sat up, ruling the Empire – alone. And in the case of the Emperor, with cheese and ham slathered over his poor, aching feet.

209 AD

13.

EBORACUM

When we arrived at Eboracum, the cold rain was drizzling down like walls of grey that hid the town completely. Our carriage stuck in the mud, and the oxen skidded on slippery cobblestones. The river was so high that at first we could not cross it and had to wait around while the carriage was dug out, freezing and dripping and miserably cursing the fate that had dragged us to this horrible place. Even when we got into the town, we saw nothing of Eboracum except the rain for the next two days.

When we finally did get to see it, it was a

disappointment. Londinium had been a proper Roman city; Lindum was a centre for trade with a busy feeling about it. But Eboracum was just an army camp, it seemed, with run-down defences. It had been built, Marcus told me, to split the territory of two tribes, the Parisi and the Brigantes, and you could tell it was a fortress. Everyone in Eboracum was there, in one way or another, because of the soldiers.

By now, I was tired of soldiers. I was tired of the tramp-tramp-tramp of their boots and the clashing jingle of their chain mail. Tired of the blaring trumpets. Even the scarlet banner and the gilded eagles hurt my eyes. I missed the sunshine, I missed the grapes and sweet figs that I had taken for granted in Leptis Magna, I missed the grand buildings of Rome, and I missed the clever conversations my father and his friends had late into the evening when the air was scented with blossom. Here, there seemed to be no flowers, no blossom, no colour that wasn't drab grey-green or the blaring scarlet and gold of the soldiers, and the main smell was the river: cool and damp at best, and stinking at worst. *British rivers and marshes, I thought, were a poor exchange for living on the brink of the fresh, wild sea which always smelled clean.*

But it was clear that the Emperor had big plans for Eboracum. After all, it was now the most important town in the Empire – for the head of the Empire was wherever the Emperor was.

"From now on, Eboracum will be the capital of Britannia Inferior," the Emperor told the assembled officials. A ripple of pride and excitement ran through the crowd. He had the defences repaired and improved, timber walls replaced with stone and he had new buildings set up, to make it all more Roman. The message to all who lived here – the soldiers of Rome, the British tribesmen who wore togas and spoke Latin, the Gaulish traders and their Punic wives, their children with blue eyes and tanned skin who played in the river's shallows – was: *This too is Rome, and we are here to stay.*

Except the Emperor, it became clear, was not here to stay for long.

For the first evenings in Eboracum, I had nothing to do but sit in my room, listen to the rain, and read or weave and wait for Julia Domna to remember my existence and send for me. It was very boring, for there was no one of my own age, and my father, who would gladly have had me stay with a respectable family in the city, was kept so busy by the Emperor that he had not a moment to arrange it. I got nervous and unhappy and could not stop thinking of my mother, my old nurse and even of Publius. I was fifteen now. I wondered what would happen to me.

Then, just before midnight, my father came into my bedroom, where I was dozing in a chair. I did not like to go to bed before I knew he was home. He was accompanied by his slave, Salvius, whom he had bought in Lindum.

"Camilla?" His face was pale, but perhaps that was just the light from the oil lamp. His voice sounded calm enough.

"Yes, Father?"

"Pack anything of value you have. The Emperor travels to the Northern borders tomorrow."

I sat up, wide awake suddenly, as Salvius began silently packing my father's belongings.

"The borders? You mean the wall?"

"Yes, to retake the wall that the emperors before Commodus built."

"Will it... be dangerous?" I said as I began to collect my personal belongings.

"I hope so! I may finally get my barbarian to dissect," he said cheerfully.

"I meant – for us."

"Us?" He shook his head. "Camilla, you don't understand. I am to travel with the Emperor to the wall in the North. You are to remain here, with the

Empress. You are packing to move into the Empress's apartments."

I leapt to my feet.

"Father, no! You can't leave me here alone!"

"You won't be alone. You will live with the Empress."

"But—"

He glanced at Salvius, then ushered me out of the room and into his own room. In a low voice, he said: "Camilla, I know this is frightening to you, but you will be safe here. You cannot possibly follow the army up North. I would not be able to take care of you and things are different up there. It may well be dangerous, for us as well as the barbarians. But we will soon be home again, and you will be safe with the Empress."

"Is Caracalla going?"

"Yes, and Geta is staying here to rule in place of his father. The Empress knows you are a clever, good girl. You can make yourself useful to her – but don't make yourself too useful. You understand."

I understood. I did not want to know the Empress's secrets. It would put me in danger.

My father opened his medicine chest. It was a wooden chest, decorated with a carving of the holy serpents of Asclepius. Inside were many compartments, full of the most extraordinary and rare things: venoms and bitumens, spices and dried dungs. He mixed these together in his pestle and mortar to create the cures that amazed people. In every city we had visited, he had been to the market, bargaining with the traders about things he had a shortage of. I knew the uses of some of his medicines, but not all of them.

"I'll leave you some of my stock," he told me, measuring some of his medicines out into smaller pouches and wraps. "Diphryges, that's for nasty tumours. And a small, very small amount of theriac, against poison. Don't waste that. It is for emergencies only. You are no doctor, but you are a sensible girl and you have learned a lot from me. Be worthy of the education you have received."

"Thank you, Father, I will," I replied sincerely.

This made things different. I was not being left behind like a useless lump of luggage. I was being left with a skill – with work to do.

14.

AVITORIA

The Empress herself gave me a medicine chest. It was a silver box, with the staff of Asclepius worked on the lid, the snakes curling around the staff. On the sides, the figures of Hercules and Dionysus were engraved, because the box had been made in Leptis Magna. It was the most expensive thing I had ever owned, and looking at the gods of my home made me feel homesick.

"Perhaps you have the skill of your father," the Empress told me. I hoped I had. I did not want to disappoint her – or her slaves, who had come to rely on me to take care of their health.

My first job, however, was nothing to do with medicine.

The Empress's hair was styled every day by a team of slaves who had been trained in the latest methods. For an hour daily, she sat in her chair while three women worked like architects to create a crowning glory for her. Finally they decorated it with gilt, ivory and glass hairpins, which sparkled like a halo when the light touched them. Other slaves applied her make-up, the scented creams and perfumes. These all came in glass or gold pots and vessels, inlaid with patterns or images of serpents or birds. Finally they draped her in her silk stola and the woollen shawl she wore now that we were in cold Eboracum. All this time, she dictated her letters and notes to me, and I did my best to take down every word, in Greek or Latin.

But illness comes suddenly to everyone, and one day the hairdressers were all sick: feverish and vomiting. I arrived to find the Empress as upset as I had ever seen her.

"Camilla," she greeted me at once, "take the slave Aisopos and go out and find me a hairdresser."

She must have seen the hesitation on my face, for she added, annoyed: "You have been here every day. You have seen exactly how I like my hair. Go and find someone who can dress it as well as my slaves, or I'll have the three of them beaten. Go!"

I went. Aisopos was an elderly lame Ethiop who looked after the Empress's petty cash. I had treated him for fever before, on several occasions. He was clearly as doubtful as I was of the wisdom of sending me to find a hairdresser, but there was no going against the Empress's orders. I put on my heavy shoes and cloak for the streets and, with Aisopos following close behind me, set out into Eboracum in search of someone who could do hair the way they did it in Rome.

Where should I look for a hairdresser? I wondered. I turned away from the smelly, noisy streets where the potters and the smiths and the leatherworkers lived, and instead headed towards the forum. I led the way hesitantly, occasionally glancing at Aisopos in hopes of a hint. I didn't want to ask him – after all he was the slave, I was supposed to be in charge – but he caught my eye. I raised my eyebrows hopefully, and he widened his and looked completely blank. Clearly he too had no idea where to find a high-class hairdresser in a city full of soldiers.

I prayed under my breath to Fortune to guide my footsteps, and she must have listened, for as I passed the marketplace, I ran full-tilt into a blonde girl, who cried out and dropped the basket she was carrying. Out clattered hairpins, polished mirrors, combs, ribbons, false hair, and all kinds of other things.

"Fool of a child!" she burst out, and then spotted the richness of my dress and the fact I was followed by a slave. Her eyes widened and she ducked down as if to avoid a blow, and hastily collected her things back into her basket.

"You're a hairdresser!" I exclaimed.

"One of the best," she replied cautiously. "I belong to Theodora."

I had no idea who Theodora was, though I did think it was an unusual name – Greek. I did not care, however. I grabbed all her fallen goods and returned them to the basket as fast as I could. Baffled, she stared at me.

"Come with me," I told her. "If you're really as good as you say, the Empress will make you and your mistress rich, and I hope I will live another day!"

We hurried back through the streets to the palace. She had seemed a little doubtful at first, but a coin from Aisopos had convinced her that whoever we were, we could pay. The girl was older than me, I guessed, but not by many years. I noticed she was pretty, and she was polite and obedient, but there was a sadness in her face that nothing I said to reassure her seemed to cut through – there was a dullness in her eyes, which were the blue of a spring sky. Her name was Avitoria.

We burst triumphantly – well, Aisopos and I were triumphant – into the portico of the palace, and the doors opened for us. We crossed the courtyard and I went into the Empress's apartments. I heard Geta's voice from outside and hesitated.

"But, Mother, I have no idea how to answer this peasant," he was saying, petulantly. "Does an emperor worry about who owns some miserable strip of land not even fit for farming? Why should I waste my time on this?"

"Because, my son, this is the business of governing the Empire," the Empress said patiently. "One day, you and your brother will do this together."

Geta's snort was audible through the panels of the door, and I stepped back hastily. "Together! I will do nothing together with that man. I know that he has been taken off to the North because the soldiers prefer me – to try and make him look like a soldier when we all know he's nothing but a murderer who cannot control his passions."

"Geta!" The Empress's voice was sharp. Halfway through her next sentence Geta yanked the door open and strode out. I was glad I had moved aside. He stormed off and I dared to lead Avitoria inside.

Luckily, she was as good as she had promised. Her fingers flew through the Empress's hair as skilfully as a woman weaving a patterned cloth, and the frown on the Empress's face softened, line by line erasing as the waves were smoothed out and plumped up and curled. When the glittering crown of hairpins was finally perfect, she stood up with a smile.

"You may tell your mistress you will serve me from

now on," she told the slave girl. "Every day, be here before daybreak."

Avitoria bowed in acknowledgement. Our eyes met and I smiled at her, thrilled to have succeeded in the task for the Empress, but she just looked back at me without returning the smile, her eyes flat, as if long ago a veil had dropped over them that she had decided never to raise again.

"Why did you smile at her? She was just a slave," you say.

It shocks me a little. We have two slaves on the farm, Caledonians born into slavery. I think we treat our slaves well – we feed them the same food we eat, we free them when we can and they are never beaten. They can live together, have possessions, have children. Almost every slave we have freed has chosen to stay here, to farm the pieces of land we have given them. My father always taught me that to free a slave without giving them a means of feeding themselves is just a slow way of murdering them.

But enslaved is still enslaved.

"I suppose I was lonely," I say. "There was no one else of my age around, and. . ." I tail off.

"It doesn't matter," you say, bored already. "What happened next?"

I look down the hill. Avitoria was a Caledonian. But she had not been born into slavery. She knew what it was like to live free.

I take a deep breath and go on with the story.

15.

THE HAIRDRESSERS
ON THE TOP FLOOR

Yes, it was stupid, but I tried to be friends with Avitoria.

At home, you see, I had grown up alongside the children of trusted slaves who knew they would be freed in due course. But now I was living at the court of the most powerful and sophisticated and cruel people in the Empire. I had lost my home, my mother, given my childhood doll to the gods. My father might never come back. I was a toy for Julia Domna – I amused her by reading to her, by holding her wool while she wove, by taking dictation of her less important notes, by listening for hours on end to her telling me about the life of mystics of the East. She believed in magic and ate up stories of miracles hungrily. Every

123

day she worshipped Heliogabalus, the sun god of the mountains, whose priestess she was. Geta too joined in these rites. Myself, I longed for our own household gods. I did my devotions to the household gods of the Emperor, but it was not the same.

Over the months that passed, letters came often from my father, written on sheets of wood. That was strange to me; I had expected them on wax tablets. The Empress's censors read them first, as usual, but then passed them on to me. They would not have found them disturbing. My father wrote kindly, with lots of Stoic morals and recommended reading, and I wrote back reassuringly, and nothing was said or asked about how the campaign in the North was progressing. In the Empress's household, I was supposed to be safe and looked after – and I was in a way; I lacked for nothing, not food or drink or clothes. But I was often forgotten completely, like a pet that does not really belong to anyone. One day, it was my birthday, and no one noticed.

"Avitoria!" I called her as she came out of the Empress's room. She looked at me, startled.

"Today is my birthday," I told her. "Will you share some honey cakes with me after you finish dressing the Empress's hair? It will be fun!" I hesitated as I saw she did not seem pleased or excited. If anything, she looked frightened and worried.

"Do you fear your mistress?" I asked kindly. "I will come back with you if you like, if the Empress allows it, and speak to her."

She did smile then, finally.

"You are kind to me," she said slowly, in her strange Caledonian accent.

I shrugged, feeling awkward. To be told I was kind reminded me that she was not Livia. It made me uncomfortable.

Taking a household slave with me, I went with Avitoria through the streets of Eboracum. Until now, I had not given a thought to where Avitoria lived. She led me away from the forum, down narrow, dirty streets, where rainwater pooled in front of rooms that backed onto the shops and taverns. People watched curiously and I began to feel uncomfortable.

Avitoria stopped by a small door and knocked. A stray cat slipped by my ankles, and I jumped. I heard footsteps from inside. Avitoria called out in a language I did not understand.

The door was opened hesitantly by another woman, who looked to be from the same tribe as her. They exchanged whispers and glanced at me uncertainly. I blushed. I had begun to realise I had done something foolish. The imperial household slave stood primly by the door, clearly thinking I was as foolish as I thought myself.

After a few moments, a tall, elegant woman, about the age my mother had been when she died, came to the door. She wore a worried frown, but I was astonished when she greeted me in the language of my own city, Punic. On her wrist she wore two bangles: one white ivory, one black jet.

I fumbled the words at first, it having been so long since I had spoken it, and she switched easily to Greek. Her name was Theodora and Avitoria was her slave.

"Do you have no mother, child?" she said, looking at me with sympathy as she led me into the house.

The words made tears well up and I had to swallow. It had been a long time since I had been asked about my mother.

I quickly saw that the two rooms Avitoria and the other slaves shared with their mistress were smaller than my own apartments. Theodora offered me food and drink, and out of good manners I had to accept, although I could see she had something on her mind and would have preferred me to go. She kept glancing towards the back room, as if there was something there that troubled her.

She told me she was a Greek freedwoman from Apollonia, who had married a Gaulish soldier. After he had died she had had to support herself and had a knack for copying hairstyles easily. Now she owned several

126

slaves, like Avitoria, whom she had taught to dress hair with the same skill she had.

"I have been busy since the Empress arrived here," she said with a smile. "Everyone wants their hair to be just like hers!"

From the back room came a moan of pain.

"Is someone ill?" I asked.

"One of my girls dropped a glass jar and has hurt her foot badly," she explained. "We have bound up the wound, but she is in a lot of pain. Forgive her, miss."

"May I see?" I asked.

Theodora looked startled. "If you wish."

I went to the bedroom and greeted the girl who was lying on the bed. The bandage was already coming undone, and as soon as I saw it I knew I would have to do something. I had never treated a wound like this before, but I had seen my father do it often enough.

"Can you bring me old wine and clean linen cloths?" I said to Theodora. I began unwrapping the bandage. Theodora looked as if she was going to object, but Avitoria quickly whispered in her ear, and she nodded.

I undid the bandage, talking calmly and reassuringly to the girl as I did so. Her name was Vitia and she was an Ethiop, like Aisopos. We were able to talk about the port of Leptis Magna, where she had been bought by the Gaulish captain of a ship. I saw at once that the wound was cut across the muscle, and not downwards. My heart sank. It would never heal like this.

"It needs stitching," I told Theodora as soon as she came back. "Do you have clean cat gut and a needle?"

Vitia flinched back, her eyes wide with fear. As soon as she understood that the muscles would not join up properly without the stitches, however, she bravely prepared herself. I gave her as much of the wine to drink as she needed to dull her pain, and used the rest to clean the wound. Then, forcing my fingers not to shake, I quickly put in four stitches to seal the wound up.

"There!" I said cheerfully, tying a knot. My father had told me how important it was to make the patient feel that all was well. "All done and it will soon heal as good as new now."

I was relieved when Vitia slipped into a deep, exhausted sleep, with no fever. But I had not expected Theodora's gratitude. She kissed my hands, and I felt embarrassed. I had only done what my father had shown me.

"The slaves are like my daughters," she told me. "I was once like them. When I die, I want them to go free, but not to beg their bread – as skilled hairdressers they can earn their own living."

Theodora begged me to come to her house whenever I could, after that. I agreed – as long as the Empress did not need me. The girls caught fevers and other illnesses as regularly as anyone – but if they were ill, they could not work, she could not earn, and no one ate. They were so grateful to find someone who would treat them for free that they soon forgot how young I was. And I was not so young after all, any more. As the weeks turned into months, I worried more and more about what would become of me. What if my father never came back from the North?

It was at Theodora's house that I met Arcturus.

I arrived one day with Ganymede, a young slave of Theodora's. He and Avitoria had taken a liking to each other and spent their time whispering and giggling together. It irritated me, but I put up with it because I could not walk through the streets without an escort. I wanted Avitoria to notice me, not Ganymede, who made her blush and brought a little sparkle to her veiled blue eyes. I knew it was foolish of me and that made me even crosser – with myself and with Avitoria. She did not even seem to notice, and that was even more irritating. Still, my heart fluttered whenever I heard her voice as she came to open the door for us.

This time, however, it was not Avitoria who opened the door, but a strange boy a few years older than me.

He was dark-haired and blue-eyed, and to my surprise he was dressed like a farmer, not in an elegantly draped toga but in those odd, bulky trousers that Celts like, with a *birrus Britannicus*, a hooded cloak that was popular with the barbarians, worn over it. I have never been good at disguising my feelings – everything shows on my face. I must have smirked. He scowled and called: "Theodora!" He had the voice of a farmer too, made for yelling across fields at cows, and a strong British accent.

"My brother-in-law's son, Arcturus," Theodora explained as she came to join us. "He has come into town to sell some heifers."

Cows – so I had been right.

"I think the young lady can see I'm not usually to be found in the theatre or admiring the sound of my own voice in the basilica," said Arcturus dryly.

"I am certainly not used to seeing men without a toga," I retorted, feeling a bit stung, as the theatre and the basilica described my father well.

"A toga is a lovely garment, but a little impractical for ploughing a muddy field or tramping through undergrowth after a lost sheep," he replied.

"True, it's meant for civilisation," I said. His air of superiority was annoying. What did he have to swagger about? He still had mud on his boots, after all. And I could definitely smell the farmyard.

"Ah yes, I always forget how you Romans love cities," he answered. "Strange, for your wealth all comes from the countryside."

"You are Roman too," Theodora put in, clearly concerned by the fact that we had just met and were instantly, it seemed, arguing.

"*British*-Roman!" said Arcturus firmly. I did know what he meant. I felt like a provincial too, as foreign in Rome as I was in Britain. But I couldn't understand why he was so obsessed with the countryside. There was nothing there – just bleak, wild, boring danger. Everything that mattered was in the cities.

He left soon after that. Theodora looked weary and worried, and I asked her if it was something to do with Arcturus. She smiled and shook her head.

"He really is a good boy," she told me. "He comes every time he visits town to check that I am all right. He just dislikes cities so much – he is happiest on his farm."

"It must be a special place," I said, trying to make up for my behaviour. I did feel I had been rude.

"It is, but hard to make a living – it's not like Italy, where crops grow so easily. There's little sun and the wind cuts through you to the bone. It's in Brigante country, north of here – his mother is from the Brigante tribe and his father is the brother of my dead husband.

131

They have been there twenty years since Gaius received his pension and land, and settled down there. His father is still working for the Empire in a sense – guarding his wife's relatives in case they revolt."

That was all we said about Arcturus. But now and then I bumped into him, on market day, and though we rarely exchanged more than a few casual words we smiled more often, as if wanting to make up for the unpleasant way in which we had met.

211 AD

16.

Bad News

The Emperor had been in the North for more than a year. We heard regular news, which was reassuring in one way – the Caledonians and Maetae had been roundly driven back, and the Antonine Wall had been retaken. The defences were being rebuilt on Hadrian's Wall. We were safe. But what I heard in the gossip at the market was another matter.

I was with Avitoria, going to her mistress's house to let the blood of a Gaulish slave who was anxious to have it done. I had only done blood-letting once before, and I was very nervous, knowing how easily it could go wrong.

So, when Avitoria suddenly stopped still, eyes wide, I was cross with her.

"What is it? Have you seen your love, Ganymede?" I said crossly.

She threw me a glance of such bitterness that I was silent. "Listen," she hissed at me.

I listened, but all I heard was the babble of British words, as there often was on market day. The Ordovices, the Brigantes, the Catuvellauni – all had different accents and dialects, and it was exhausting to listen to so many conversations that I did not understand. I did pick out some words though: 'Caledonians', 'massacre', and – I shivered – 'Caracalla'.

I took Avitoria's hand and together we moved slowly and unnoticed through the crowd, just a young woman out shopping with her slave. I could feel the blood pulsing in her wrist, too fast. I stopped by one of the public water spouts and she drank deeply. Her face was pale.

"What has happened?" I asked, though I already had my suspicions.

She swallowed.

"The Emperor is not well. He has returned to Hadrian's Wall and sent his son Caracalla to conquer my people. But. . . it seems he has murdered them. Women. Children. Everyone."

It had been a long time since I had seen Caracalla. But I could believe every word. The Emperor was a soldier. Caracalla was a murderer. There was a difference.

"Your family. . ." I said.

"I don't know. They may be dead now. Oh, I wish I could know. I was only a child when I was taken. I would do anything to be free, so I could try to find them, even if I only find their bones."

It was a terrible thing for a slave to say, but I could not find it in my heart to blame her. Instead I reached out to touch her hand in sympathy. But before I could do so, she moved swiftly away, and I was left hurrying after her, trying not to lose her in the crowd.

From that day on, Avitoria's interest in me disappeared like a shadow under the rising sun. She barely gave me a glance, instead spending all the time she could whispering with Ganymede in corners. I was hurt and humiliated and angry, but how could I object? They were slaves. I was free. They were not even *my* slaves, so I could not free them. I cried myself to lonely sleep every night, knowing how stupid I was being, unable to stop feeling things Roman women in stories – Lucretia or Lavinia – would have scorned to feel. I read the *Aeneid* over and over again, especially the part about

135

Dido, who promised to be faithful to her dead husband, but fell in love with Aeneas by the will of Venus. She killed herself when Aeneas sailed on to his destiny to found Rome. Dido and Cleopatra, Punic and Egyptian, were unable to conquer their passions, and were destroyed by them. Miserably, I felt that, like them, I was an Eastern woman, not Roman enough, lacking in virtue, dignity and piety. I did not understand my own feelings. I only knew that Avitoria was unhappy, and so was I.

Then one day Julia Domna said something that made me realise what all the whispering was about.

"When will that Theodora sell you to me?" she said to Avitoria casually, as Avitoria carefully curled and lifted up her hair into the rolls she loved so much.

A hairpin fell from Avitoria's hand. One of the other girls pounced on it and handed it back to her.

"I do not know, my Empress," she said quietly, setting the pin in its place.

"Tell her I will pay well. You have skilful hands, and you work quietly, without gossiping. I like that. I expect to hear from her soon."

Now I understood what the trouble was. Theodora had made no secret of the fact that she meant to free her slaves in her will. But if Avitoria was sold to the Empress, she would never be free – she would be taken back to Rome and she would never know what had happened to her family.

"You won't be sold," I told her as soon as we were alone. "Theodora would never sell you. You are like her family."

Avitoria turned to me. She was still holding the Empress's face cream, a gold pot with a red glass snake on the lid. Her fingers were white as she clutched it.

"A request from the Empress," she said, her voice shaking, "is not a request."

I had no answer for her. We both knew it was true.

"Let me talk to the Empress," I said. "Perhaps I can appeal to her."

Avitoria looked at me gratefully. I wanted so much to be able to please her. But when I found myself alone with the Empress, my courage fled. I did not know how to open the subject. What could I say? It would look strange and suspicious to care about the fate of a slave. In the end, I tried in the evening, when she seemed calm and relaxed, and Geta was at home for once.

"My Empress, are there no hairdressers in Rome?" I said, trying to make my voice sound casual.

She looked at me in surprise. It was very rare that I spoke to her without being spoken to first.

"What do you mean?"

"I don't know why you want to take that Caledonian

back with you." It was a dangerous game I was playing, and I was horribly aware that I did not know how to play it. "Can she be trusted, after all?" I said weakly. Had I said too much? I did not want to push the Empress the other way, into mistrusting Avitoria and perhaps having her killed. "She is a Caledonian."

Julia Domna frowned at me.

"Now what is your real meaning," she said to herself, a smile in her voice. "Oh, I see. You are jealous of her, aren't you? You fear I like her more than I like you?"

I was forced to nod.

"Don't concern yourself. She is just a slave, and you will no doubt be married when we return to Rome, with plenty of other things to fill your mind and time. I will find someone. . . appropriate for you."

I could not think of anything else to say. At least, I told myself, I had tried.

Later in the week, I spoke to Theodora about it too, but she just shook her head bleakly.

"I cannot refuse the Empress," she told me. "If I let her have Avitoria, at least I am safe and the other girls are safe too."

17.

SNOW

It was February, a colder day than I had ever known, and the air was sharp as a sword blade. I could not settle. I paced up and down in my room, watching the messengers go back and forth in the courtyard below.

"Camilla!" The Empress's maid called me, sounding annoyed. "Get ready, the Empress wants you to go with her to the basilica."

I dressed in a hurry. Every day, Geta was supposed to hear cases and complaints from local landowners. He was the face of the Emperor. But he hated every moment of it. As he sat in the chair in the basilica it was clear he was dropping off to sleep as the lawyers droned on. Their thick British accents mangled their speeches until it was hard even to understand what was being said. Judgements were passed and lives destroyed, and Geta yawned his way through it all. One man put his head in his hands, as the judge ordered him to sell himself into slavery to clear his debt. His family sat with blank, hopeless faces. Others were sentenced to work in the mines, for theft, and went away roaring their innocence, although the evidence had sounded conclusive enough to me. Just behind Geta sat Julia Domna. Occasionally she leaned forwards and asked an intelligent question that made the pompous lawyers sit up, startled to realise this woman was the one in real control. Then some complicated case came up, and the Empress stood up to speak privately with the officials. The conversation went on and on, and the sky outside seemed an odd colour, yellowish. Somehow, I could not rid myself from the feeling that Theodora needed me.

Just at that moment, I spotted a flash of colour by the door. My eyes widened. It was a snake. It wriggled fast across the threshold, its scales glittering, almost glowing in the dull light. For a shocked second I believed it was the snake from the Empress' face-cream pot, somehow come to life and slithering away. It had the same diamond-shaped mark on its head. Then it was gone – slipping into a black crack in the wall, vanishing like a melting snowflake.

Everyone knew that snakes were spirits, and more than spirits – visitors from the gods. I felt throughout my body that this was a sign. I stood up and, excusing myself as unwell, I snatched my cloak and went to the door. I had to get out.

As I stepped out of the basilica, something bit me. I looked up, and found myself showered in blossom – but freezing blossom. Snow! I gasped. I had seen snow before, but I never got used to how beautiful it was. I gazed in amazement at the sparkling jewels that clung to my sleeve.

"You should see it on the hills outside the city," remarked a voice.

I looked up. It was Arcturus.

"Is it even more beautiful there?" I asked.

"Yes, because no one treads it to slush. Here in the city it will be brown, dirty water by sunset, but out where my farm is... the hills glow in the moonlight like silver."

"I'd love to see that," I said, and meant it.

"Are you here alone?" he asked.

"No, but I had the feeling..." I shook my head. "I felt somehow that Theodora needed me." I explained about the snake. He understood at once and he frowned.

"Shall I take you to Theodora? Would that set your mind at rest?"

I hesitated.

"Oh, don't worry about going with me unescorted,"

he added. "People see you as a doctor now, not as a young lady – they are not surprised by it."

He meant to reassure me, and he did, but I also felt my heart sink. I had been suspecting something like this had happened to me, to the way people saw me. In Leptis Magna, I had been a child. In Rome, I had been a valuable object, a bride to be decorated richly and looked after carefully. I never left my parents' house without an escort. But here, in Britain, I was not so important any more. I could come and go like any poor woman who worked for their living. I did not think my father would be pleased with the change when he came back from the North.

"I should stay here," I said shortly. "The Empress needs me."

It was not until the next day that I was able to go to Theodora's house, and by that time the feeling of panic had gone. I could not even be sure if I had dreamed the snake. After all, a snake in winter? In the city? No, I decided, it was just my imagination.

Yet, as I arrived at the house, I saw a dead cat on the rubbish heap by the door. It was a dirty white cat with one ginger ear; I had seen it skulking around a few times before. Snow was swiftly covering it. I do not know why this struck me – dead animals were hardly a rare sight in the area. But perhaps I was in the mood to see signs from the gods. I did not spend much time looking at it then, but later on, I did remember it – and the sign from the gods.

18.

A Dream from
the Gods

That night, I dreamed of home.

In the dream, I was in the theatre in Leptis Magna. I had never actually been there, but my father had described it to me, so I knew what I was seeing. I was sitting on the topmost tier of seats, looking down at an empty stage.

The theatre was enormous, like Olympus. I felt dizzy. The marble columns on the stage were taller than the tallest trees I had ever seen, taller than pines or palms. Through them I glimpsed a line of rich blue sea behind the pillars, flecked with white-topped waves. I was perched so high that I could see the roundness of the world.

On each side of the stage stood huge statues of the Diascuri, the holy twin gods. Enormous, cast in shining bronze, they looked like real giants with tanned, sweaty skin. Their eyes were picked out in white glass and they gleamed as if they were alive. I realised that they were watching us, the audience. Except there was no audience – there was only me. Strangely, this did not disturb me, or at least, only deep in the back of my head, as if someone far away from me was shouting a warning. I knew why I was there; I was there to see a story.

My father said that dreams were very important. If someone came to him feeling unwell, one of the first things he would ask was: "What dreams have you been having?" Dreams were one of the ways in which the gods spoke to us, and Asclepius often sent cures in dreams. The great doctor, Galen, had cured his own serious illness after following the advice of a dream. So, I told myself, even in the dream, that I had to pay close attention. Whatever was being shown to me was important. But although I waited and waited, the play did not begin. The stage was empty. All I could see was the sea behind the pillars.

I began to feel as though something was wrong. As the shadows lengthened, the Diascuri seemed to frown at me.

I gripped the cold marble edge of my seat, frightened. Even the sea seemed shadowed, although there were no clouds in the sky. Then, I realised that it was not a shadow. It was a wave – a huge wave the length of the entire horizon. It was coming towards me, and growing fast.

I leapt to my feet. A distant rumble and crash told me it had hit the shore. Spray flew up in the air, with shards of stone, brick and dust. Where there had been a forest of columns, there was suddenly just boiling sea, racing towards me faster than wild white horses.

I screamed.

The wave came, racing up through the helpless city, drowning the houses, smashing down the trees, tossing boats like blossom in the wind, spurting between columns, swamping the Diascuri, heading straight towards me. I tasted salt and felt spray in my face—

Then I woke up, my heart pounding.

The moonlight was shining straight through my window and I was soaked in sweat. My blankets were twisted and tumbled on the floor. I could hear voices and hurrying feet outside in the courtyard and wondered if I had screamed so loudly that I had woken people up. The dream had been so horribly real. I could only think of one meaning: I was going to die soon. After all, the wave had come for me and no one else in the theatre.

"I don't want to die!" I sobbed out loud.

Hooves clattered outside in the courtyard. The light was not all moonlight, I realised; some of it was torches carried by people outside. This surely wasn't all happening because of my nightmare. I jumped up and went to look out of the window.

The courtyard was full of men and horses. The men wore armour and carried flaming torches. The horses snorted and shook their harnesses till they jingled. I spotted a familiar shape, a box carried by weary slaves: the Emperor's litter. Then I heard a voice that was more than familiar.

"Father!" I gasped.

I didn't stop to think if I were dressed to go out or not, I just flung open the door, raced down the stairs and threw myself into his arms.

I was home at last.

19.

The Return

"My grandfather!" you say. "You never told me how he died."

I look down at my hands on the reins. Even now, I feel hollow and lonely when I think of my father. How can it be over twenty years since I last heard his voice? But it is.

"He died," I begin, my voice sounding strange in my own ears, "because he was murdered."

"You're back at last!" I pulled out of my father's arms, looking up at his face with delight – and my happiness vanished just as the dream had. Even in the flickering torchlight, I could see that he looked terrible. His eyes were hollow and haunted; his face was like that of a man already dead, eaten from inside.

"My daughter," he said, and kissed my forehead.

"Thank the gods you are safe. I have worried so much about you."

"What has happened, Father?" I asked in a low voice. I looked around me. The soldiers filling the courtyard were menacing as the torchlight glinted from their breastplates and helmets. Their boots and their horses had churned the snow in the courtyard to slush, and they looked wild-eyed and savage, and there was an edge in the air that I could not describe. I felt as if I were in the presence of a terrifying god, one who might swing his sword of vengeance one way or another without warning. The Emperor was nowhere to be seen, nor was the Empress. But Caracalla was there. Caracalla was dressed in travel-stained clothes and he looked older and harder-faced than before. He was glaring up the steps that led from the courtyard to the higher floors where the imperial family had their rooms. At the top of the steps, I now saw, stood Geta.

He had clearly just been woken, and he had his toga thrown over his tunic. Although he stood higher than Caracalla, there was something about the way he felt for the edge of his toga, to stop it slipping, that made it seem as though he was the weaker.

"Welcome home, brother," he said.

Caracalla did not reply. As if his silent glare was a signal, the soldiers in the courtyard separated, without words, like water and oil. Some moved towards Caracalla, and some went up the steps to join Geta. More went towards Geta, but the men who stayed with Caracalla had the look of hungry dogs about them.

I watched, frozen with terror. I actually expected one of them to attack the other at that moment, but instead, Geta glanced at my father.

"Physician," he commanded, "the Emperor needs you at once."

My father broke free from me and went after him without a word. Caracalla followed them, his gang of soldiers behind him. I was left standing and shivering in the cold shadows, with the stars above me, frightened and confused. There was nothing to do but go back to my room and wait for news. I did not go back to sleep.

At daybreak my father came to find me. In the pale light he looked worse than ever. He sat on the end of my bed and began talking. It was as if the words had been bottled up for so long that they had to spill out of him.

"At the start," he began, "it was a disaster. We marched into the wilds of Caledonia. Gods, that place is forsaken! Nothing but stinking marshes and biting insects, freezing cold winds and bleak stones, everything drab and the rain lashing down as if we were slaves under a whip. Yes, we got the Antonine Wall back, but at what cost?"

I flinched at the bitter fury in his voice.

"The Caledonians hid in the land they knew well and attacked us when we were least expecting it, vanishing away like ghosts before we could gather ourselves together to attack. We lost hundreds of men."

"But how—?" This was not the story of victory I had expected.

He gestured impatiently.

"There are no roads up there, and the ground eats people up without warning. If there weren't forests barring our way, there were freezing, treacherous rivers to bridge, and if there weren't swamps, there were sheer cliffs with an evil slippery kind of gravel that tore men off balance and hurled them to their death on sharp rocks, like teeth. Then arrows would come whizzing out of nowhere, and you'd feel as powerless as a sitting duck waiting for the hunter to strike you down. Horrible!" He paused for breath and wiped a thin sweat from his forehead. I saw his hair was greyer than it had been and shot with silver, and a new pink scar lined his forearm. "But that wasn't the worst of it. They put sheep and cattle in front of us, so the men, starving for some meat, would charge towards them to hunt them, become separated, and then be picked off by bands of warriors. When we found them, some were dead, some wounded, and the wounded we had to kill because we could do nothing for them, and if they had been captured alive it would have been the end for us. Our men were slaughtered."

"But you took back the wall!" I cried out, shocked and eager to get some bit of hope back from what he had said. Half my mind was also racing on what this meant for Avitoria. Had the Caledonians been more successful than was rumoured? Could her parents still be alive?

"Yes, and took back the forts Julius Agricola built so many years ago – but at what cost?" he repeated. "And then the Emperor could go on no longer, even though he was being carried for most of the way in a litter, so we returned to Hadrian's Wall, and Caracalla was sent to continue the conquest."

I clutched the edge of my bed tightly. What he said next destroyed all my hopes for Avitoria.

"I would not have thought I could feel sorry for a barbarian," my father went on in a low voice. "But the women and children did not have to be killed. They could have been sold as slaves. Caracalla murdered, looted, burned… everything. He did not hold the soldiers back; instead he urged them on. When we went after him, we found nothing, no movement in the whole country. Just columns of smoke from burning bone fires, hanging in the sky. You could smell it—"

He broke off, and pushed a tear from his eye. It was the only time I had ever seen him shed a tear. He had not even wept for my mother. Whatever he had seen in the North, it had destroyed his spirit.

"Is the Emperor ill?" I managed to say.

But before he could answer, I heard soldiers calling him again. He jumped up and was gone without a word.

So began a day of restless sleeping, waking, constant whispering and angry hissed passwords in the passages. Caracalla's and Geta's men split off from each other, taking possession of different parts of the palace, and scowled at each other if they passed by chance. I did not leave the house; I did not dare leave my father alone. Every so often he came back to my room, threw himself on the bed and slept like the dead. I did not dare wake him. Everything had turned into a nightmare. Julia Domna I no longer saw at all.

It was dawn when I heard a hammering at my door. There was always someone awake at every time of day or night now, and I forced myself to get up from the chair where I was sleeping and answer it. A slave grumbled that there was someone asking for me at the street door.

"For you?" My father frowned. He accompanied me down the stairs.

To my shock, it was Arcturus. He looked pale and exhausted. Snow drifted down around him, making his hair seem grey.

"What are you doing here?" I blurted out.

"Theodora – she's not well. She has been ill for days, but tonight it is much worse. We need a doctor."

20.

A POT OF POISON

I turned to my father, wordlessly. He was the doctor, not me.

He was looking at Arcturus, and it was as if he was swiftly calculating in his mind his weight in gold, or his value. He asked him a few questions – not about Theodora, but about himself. Who was his father? Where was his farm? Arcturus answered, briefly and impatient.

"We have to hurry!" Arcturus blurted out finally. "Sir, we need your help. We can pay—"

My father smiled without humour.

"I have never taken a fee for treatment, but I cannot leave the Emperor." He looked at me, then drew me to one side.

"Do you trust this young man?" he said quietly.

It was an odd question. I looked at him in surprise. "Of course," I said without thinking.

My father nodded.

"Then you go."

"Me?" I was shocked. "But I'm not a doctor."

He was listening to raised voices from inside the palace, and what he heard seemed to make his mind up. He gripped my wrist so hard that I was silent in shock.

"Listen to me, daughter, and do as I tell you. Go and get your medicine chest. Do it swiftly and let no one see you. Get your cloak and dress warmly and take anything of value that you can easily carry. Then go with this young man and do not come back until I summon you. Do you understand?"

"But—" I began.

"Go!" he said, sounding stern but kind. Still, something in his voice scared me.

"But what about you?" I blurted.

He sighed. For a moment, he looked like my father again, the man nothing could shake or trouble, who calmly treated good news just as he treated bad.

"I have given years to serving the Emperor," he said quietly. "Whether I was right or wrong, the gods will judge. But, if I am a Roman, now is not the time to abandon my duty."

158

Then he strode off, following the lights and voices towards the apartments of the Emperor.

I did as he told me, though I was confused and frightened. I ran upstairs and put all my possessions into the silver chest that the Empress had given me. I did not have much. There was a hush all over the palace, but I felt as if no one was asleep. It felt more as if everyone was awake, listening, waiting and watching. I wondered if Caracalla had something planned. As I hurried back through the palace to the door where Arcturus was waiting, I glimpsed a few frightened faces peeping from behind doors. The doors shut as soon as I got close to them.

"What's happening in there?" Arcturus demanded as I stepped out with him into the snow.

"I don't know. I hope my father will be all right."

"Thank you for coming," he said, and I could hear in his voice that he meant it. "There is no one of our family here but me, and I have no skills in medicine."

I did not reply. I wished I had his faith in me, but I knew that the small store of medicines I had in the box was not going to work miracles. Only the gods could do that.

Eboracum in the pale light of dawn was menacing and silent. A few men slipped from shadow to shadow, watching us and sometimes following us for a few blocks. A few carts rumbled through the streets, and threw up the filthy melted snow on my cloak. I could hear whispering voices and the clash and jangle of soldiers' armour. It seemed that the feeling I had sensed in the courtyard, the nervous terror, had spilled out into the city too.

"Like I said, she has been ill for days," Arcturus told me as we went on. "Low in mood, no appetite."

"How many days?"

"Since last market day at least. That's when I arrived, as usual. I could see she was not well, so I stayed. She got worse and worse. I have called in doctors, but nothing they did has worked – they bled her, they gave her medicines. So I thought, perhaps the Emperor's own doctor. . ."

We reached the house, where a frightened-looking Vitia was standing by the open door ready to welcome us in. A light was burning in the back room, and I went straight in.

As soon as I saw Theodora, lying on her bed, I knew she was far beyond my help. Her lips were pale and dry and her eyes rolled back. Still, I took an oil lamp, knelt down and tried to make her understand me.

"Can you speak, Theodora? What do you feel?"

Vitia came forward timidly.

"She has not been herself. She said she felt sad, then

she complained of stomach aches and of tingling in her limbs. She could not sleep, but instead she seemed half asleep in the daytime, slurring her words as if she were drunk – though I know she never touches wine."

"And she said she could not see properly," added another girl.

I stood up again. This was too serious for me. If there was to be any chance of saving Theodora, I knew I had to get a proper doctor, one from the palace who would know what they were doing. By now the sun was up, but the city was still oddly quiet. I looked around for Avitoria – she was known at the palace. She was hanging back, in the shadows by the door. I went to her. She looked at me with a strange, almost frightened expression in her eyes. I was not surprised she was afraid. Her mistress was dying.

"Avitoria," I told her, "go back to the palace with Arcturus and tell my father that we need a proper doctor. He must come, or send someone. The Emperor has a hundred doctors, surely one can be spared to save Theodora. Go!"

She hesitated, then nodded and hurried to the door. Arcturus followed.

I watched her go down the steps. As I did so, I thought of the theriac. It was a complex medicine that I did not know how to prepare. It was meant for emperors, and the cost of it was enormous. But it was supposed to be good for anything, and this was an emergency. Once I had thought of the theriac, I knew I could not rest until I had at least tried it.

I went back in to Theodora. There was more daylight now, coming through the high, small window. I measured out a grain of theriac and opened her lips to feed it in. She did not even flinch. In the growing light, I noticed her gums. They did not look normal. There was a blue line along them, almost like the line left by the tide when it goes out.

My heart began beating very fast. I felt that I was on the brink of something, some discovery, but I did not know what it was.

Aware of the girls watching me intently, I began to search the room. I did not really know what I was looking for, but somewhere, somehow, I thought, there had to be some clues.

"What did she eat last night?" I asked.

"Nothing, she had no appetite."

"She ate nothing at all?"

"The last thing she ate was a pie that Avitoria bought her from the pastry shop, a few days ago," said Vitia. "But when people are ill from food, that is different, isn't it?"

"Very different," I said.

162

"She had a little ale," one of the British girls, Regina, said. "Avitoria saw to it, because we were working."

I looked at the tankard that was on the table. I picked it up and held it in the daylight. It was hard to tell in the darkness, but I thought I could see a little white powder on the rim – and caught the scent of roses.

I turned and ran out of the house, my heart thumping, feeling sick. I went over to the rubbish heap. I searched the snow-covered pile for the dead cat I had seen weeks ago. It was nothing but a few scraps of fur and bone now. Under the bone, something winked and glinted in the dawn light.

I bent to pick it up. It was a cosmetic pot made of gold, inlaid with red glass in the shape of a snake. I recognised it at once. Only one woman in this town had anything so beautiful: Julia Domna, the Empress. The cosmetic pot was the one in which she kept the white lead which she used for lightening her skin.

It can poison, even as far as death. I remembered my father's words clearly, his towering rage back in Rome, my mother's exasperation. *But even the Empress uses it!*

She did. And the last time I had seen this pot was in Avitoria's hand. Now here it lay, outside her house – and inside, her mistress Theodora lay poisoned and on the brink of death.

*

"Avitoria poisoned Theodora?" you say, shocked.

I nodded. "I think so."

"But why? She was a kind mistress. She was going to free her in her will!"

"She was — until Julia Domna arrived. The Empress wanted to buy Avitoria from Theodora. I believe Avitoria decided she could not bear being sold away from her home, and lose any chance of reaching her family again. She decided to do something about it. If Theodora died before she could sell her, Avitoria would be free."

"So, she was a murderess!" you say, full of pious rage. "Of course, you told the Emperor?"

I take a deep breath, and go on.

21.

EMPEROR'S END

Standing there on the rubbish heap in Eboracum, a thousand thoughts swirled around my head. I knew in my heart that Avitoria had poisoned Theodora. I also knew the punishment for slaves who killed their owner: every slave in the household would be put to death. The girls who were hoping for their freedom tonight would be executed instead, though they had committed no crime.

For the Roman philosophers, there was no question of the right action. I should tell at once. But I was not a Roman philosopher. I was only a girl from the provinces.

I could not do it. I could not tell what I knew.

Yet I knew it was my duty to.

I still had not decided when I stepped down from

the rubbish heap, the cosmetic pot clutched in my hand. In the light of dawn, I found myself facing Avitoria. Her eyes went to the glinting pot in my hand. I saw her expression shift. Did she guess what I knew? Should I confront her? I was still so stunned by what I had discovered that I doubted myself. Perhaps I was wrong.

So it was Avitoria who spoke first – and changed everything.

"You have to go," she blurted out. I saw now that she had tears streaking her face.

"Go, where?" I said blankly.

"Anywhere, away from here!"

"I don't understand," I began. "Where is Arcturus?"

"Oh, I didn't wait for *him*. I just ran! The Emperor is dead, and Caracalla is killing everyone who was his friend," she said.

"What? Where is my father?" I gasped.

She hesitated.

"Your father had to escape. He says he will meet you outside the walls of Eboracum. He spoke of a healing spring, east of here. The waters there are sacred to Sulis. He says he will meet you there."

Then Avitoria was pulling me away from the house. It did not cross my mind to disbelieve her – there was truth in her voice and I knew in my heart it was exactly what Caracalla would do. He hungered like a wolf for power, and once he had it, he would destroy everything that might challenge that power. Geta would be lucky to survive the night, I knew – it would depend on if his mother could protect him. The palace was gone, lost to me. It had vanished like a dream. This was what my dream had foretold: not my death, but the death of Leptis Magna's most powerful son, the Emperor Septimius Severus.

Avitoria pushed me out into the street, and we went stumbling together, hand in hand, along it. The snow had all turned to dirty water now, and ran along the gutters, down towards the drains. The sun was rising. Soon there would be nowhere for me to hide. My only hope now was to meet my father. We would be penniless, beggars in a foreign land, but at least we would be alive. I stopped as I saw the gates and the guards in front of them.

"How do I get out of the city?" I said, in panic.

"You can cross the river," Avitoria said.

I realised she was right. In many places there were no walls, there was just the river. There had been laws against building fortified cities, in case they were occupied by enemies who held them against the Empire. Now the enemy *was* the Empire, I realised. Gaps between emperors loomed like chasms for the ordinary people like us. They were dangerous times.

I could hear cries and clashing swords in the distance. There was confusion, and people were shouting. Some were shouting for Caracalla, others for Geta.

"Go now," Avitoria hissed at me. "While they are all distracted."

She took her own cloak from her shoulders, and pushed it into my hands. It was thick, rough, heavy wool.

"You'll need it more than me. Go!" She squeezed me into a brief, hard hug, then pushed me away.

I knew I had no time to say anything else to her. I ran. I ducked down beside a cart that had stopped by the river, and dropped down to the riverbank. It was muddy and clammy and cold as a frog's back.

I remembered, then, how I had tried to swim from the shipwreck. My clothes had dragged me down. I tucked my skirts up and stepped into the river, keeping to the shadows. The shock of the cold was like a sword's blow to my legs. I had to bite my lip to stop myself shouting out. Then I waded out into the water, pushing ice away with my hands.

My legs ached with pain. I could not stop myself shivering and my teeth chattering. I thought I would die of the cold, but I kept wading, and finally, I pulled myself out onto the bank. My legs were like red lumps of marble. I forced myself to rub some blood back into my legs, though all I wanted was to lie down and sleep forever. Then I began walking, clumsily at first, and finally, as my aching legs woke up, running.

I did not take the road. I knew that if anyone came searching for me, it would be the roads they would search first. Instead, I pushed through undergrowth, flinching at every noise for terror I would wake a wild beast. I did not dare to go too far from the road in case I was lost in the marshes.

That night I spent huddled under a bush, drifting in and out of sleep. If it had not been for Avitoria's cloak, I think I would have frozen to death. When I woke, I peered out onto the road. Day was dawning and there was no sound of violence from the city. No one seemed to be coming after me, but nor could I see my father.

With no idea what I should do next, I began walking again – away from the city, north, hoping to find the spring. I kept imagining that I heard hoofbeats following me, racing soldiers. I was so frightened that I left the road again, and headed out into the countryside. My legs were humming with exhaustion and I felt light-headed. Snow began to fall again, first lightly and then more and more. The world whirled white ahead of me. I could see nothing, my eyelashes clogged up with ice.

As I stumbled through the snow, I seemed to dream that my mother was walking next to me. I knew it was just a dream, but I let myself enjoy it all the same.

I closed my eyes and heard the swish of her dress, the sound of her voice, the distant pleasant home-like sounds of Leptis Magna—

My eyes flew open and I just caught myself as I fell forward. I had been walking in my sleep and I seemed to have climbed a hill. Night was falling and I had caught myself just before I fell face-forward into the snow. I sat down and went to clutch my knees with bruised fingers. That was when I realised I was still holding the snake pot. I knotted it into a corner of the cloak.

I could see far from here. It looked as if the sun was rising in the distance, but I realised that was impossible, for it was setting in the west. I stared at the red light below me, staining the low cloud like blood. It was not the sun. It was a funeral pyre. Soldiers surrounded it, their armour glinting. Golden eagle standards blazed against the bone-fire flames, and the fire cast monstrous shadows onto the snow. Swords clashed on shields, and voices roared. The fire crumpled into ash, and collapsed, like Troy falling into destruction.

As I watched, an eagle circled the burning funeral pyre three times, then lifted into the sky, bathed in gold from the sunset.

"Farewell, Septimius Severus," I whispered to myself. "Now you are a god."

22.

SPRINGS OF SULIS

I stumbled down from the hill in the dawn, heading still further north. I did not know where I was going, nor did I know how long I could continue. I dreamed as I walked, of voices that had been dead a long time. And I dreamed I was arguing with Avitoria, shouting at her, accusing her of murdering Theodora.

"Camilla! Camilla!" My mother was calling me, in the distance. "This way!"

I blundered after her voice. I almost thought I could see her, like a wisp of mist on the edge of a cliff. If I ran just a little bit faster, reached just a little bit further, I could touch her.

"Ma!"

I flung myself forwards, my arms stretched out to hug her. But the look on her face was so sad. She turned away from me and melted just as my fingers touched her. I fell forwards and my foot slipped on a rock that was suddenly smooth as glass. I found myself slithering down into a gully.

I ended up, bruised and shivering, on the brink of a clear stream that ran through a cool, green cleft. It was still running despite the winter's cold. Around it, the rocks were frozen with a skin of ice. Icicles had formed, like jewels dripping from the Empress's neck.

I dipped my hand into the water and drank as deeply as I could. Then I began following the stream downwards, over the steep, slippery rocks, clinging to the bushes that grew out of the cracks to steady myself. I felt as if I had been here before, perhaps in a dream, because I seemed to know the way. Then I was clambering straight down into a small green valley, where the water fell into a natural stone bowl and disappeared into a black crack in the rocks.

I could feel that this place was sacred to the gods, but I was too tired to feel fear. I sat on the stones, dozing in and out of sleep. After some time, I noticed there were metal sheets in the water. Some glinted like gold. I could read some of the Latin as the water flowed over them. *'Cure my son who cannot walk, goddess!'* and *'I give thanks to the goddess who made me see again.'*

I looked up and saw that all around the spring,

tucked into niches and in clefts in the stone, were little models of hands, ears, feet, eyes and other parts of the body. *This must be a healing spring*, I thought. And then, all at once, I realised this must be the spring where I was meant to meet my father.

The gods had helped me find my way here. I could do nothing now but wait. So I did.

The water danced in the stone bowl and birds fluttered in the trees. Now and then snow slid from a branch and landed with a soft thump in the clearing. The light was ghostly.

I did not know if it had been minutes, or hours, before finally the bushes parted before me. A white horse stepped through the undergrowth. The rider on its back wore the *birrus Britannicus*. He looked at me from under his snow-laden hood. It was Arcturus.

I said nothing; I was used to dreams by now. They were sent by the gods. It did not seem surprising that I should have another one, in this sacred place.

"Why have you been running from me, you fool?" he said, getting down from the horse and coming towards me. His feet crunched in the snow and dead leaves. "You could have been killed, rambling over the hills like that!"

I smiled at him dreamily. True enough, dreams sent from the gods did not usually call you a fool, but after all, I was just a girl. I probably got the dreams with rougher, less elegant language.

Arcturus picked me up and carried me to the horse. He continued complaining as he tried to seat me on it, finally wedging me in front of him. I started to think that this horse smelled, and sounded, very real. Then it lifted its tail and delivered a stream of hot urine, melting the snow beneath it. I woke up. No dream horse sent from the gods did that.

"Arcturus?!" I croaked.

"Who else? I have been following you for three days. Every time I got close you went off the road."

"I heard hoofbeats, I thought the soldiers—"

"No one is following you," he interrupted.

"My father?"

"Dead. I am sorry."

His words were blunt, but I was glad he had told me the truth. I had half-guessed it anyway. For good or ill, Avitoria was a liar. She must have known I would not leave without my father. She had told a lie to save my life. My father must have guessed this would happen; that was why he had sent me away with Arcturus – to protect me.

"Who killed him?" I whispered.

"Caracalla. He slaughtered all his father's friends before the Emperor was cold. Thirty men and more must be dead," he added bitterly.

"Geta?" It had not really sunk in yet that my father was dead.

"Not yet. The army likes him. Caracalla, Geta and Julia Domna have set off for Rome already. They want to be back at the heart of the Empire, to make sure no one tries to steal their power. Abandoning Britain, once again."

We rode up out of the small valley and slowly made our way, by hidden paths that were much older than the Roman roads, to Arcturus's farm.

"No one will betray you there," he told me as we rode. "My father has lived under several emperors – he knows what they are like."

When I first looked down on the farm from the hill, a blanket of snow lay over everything. The farm was almost invisible under it, tucked into the earth. It looked like somewhere animals lived: a place to huddle, a den or a nest, a refuge. Only the bare trees and the bare walls poked out like bones.

But when the moon rose, the hills were like silver, just as Arcturus had promised.

"And that was how you came home?" you ask.

Home, *I think. I halt the pony and look down at the farmstead beneath us.* Is this home?

Perhaps it is, now.

*

It did not feel like home at first. Not even close.

There was straw on the floor, not mosaics, and it was often stuffy with the smell of some sick animal or other brought in to recover. It was a busy place. As well as Arcturus's younger sister and brother, there were men and women who came in sometimes to help with the harvest and to herd the animals. Some were from the British tribes, but others were Gaulish, Belgae, Greek and Syrian. It was not a Roman villa, and it was not even our home in Leptis Magna. But it was a happy home, with plenty of laughter, and everyone, citizen or slave, ate at the same table.

Arcturus's father was a grizzled old centurion with twinkling eyes. I saw something of Marcus in him. His eyes did all the talking, for he never wasted a word. It took some getting used to. His wife, though, was magnificent. Tall, with long grey hair that still glinted golden in some lights, she wore a golden torc around her neck and was every inch a Brigante princess. And she rode. For British women, it turned out, rode horses. The day I saw her come galloping across the fields on her strong pony, her hair flying wild in the wind, was the day I thought that maybe there might be something in Britannia I wanted.

As I regained strength, I began to worry about what I should do next. One evening I had the chance to speak to Arcturus about it. After he brought me to the farm, he vanished for a few days. He came back carrying my silver medicine chest and the news of Theodora's death. The box he gave to me, and he did not seem to have opened it.

When no one was looking, I put the cosmetic pot into the box too, and hid it under my bed. I had not told Arcturus what I suspected about Theodora's death. I knew that if I did, he would have to seek out vengeance whether he wanted to or not, and... well, somehow, I could never bring myself to say it. I could not rid myself of the memory of Avitoria's veiled blue eyes. By now, she had gone North, I heard, and Vitia was doing well, working for the same people as before, but this time earning money she could keep and save for her future. Who would have gained if I told the truth? If I must, I will answer to the gods and the spirit of Theodora for it when I die.

"Your mother was kind to me while you were in Eboracum," I said to Arcturus after he gave me my medicine chest.

"She sees you as a sick lamb who needs feeding up," he said with a grin. "Then she'll send you out into the fields again."

"That's what I am wondering. I have some skills... I can read and write Latin and Greek. I have some ability in medicine. Do you think anyone would want to employ me?"

"A few might," he said carefully.

"But in any city, they will wonder who I am, and it will get back to the Emperor, and..." I began to panic again. "What am I to do?" The thought was there, but it was a horrible one. "In my circumstances, girls with no protection, no family, no money... sell themselves into slavery."

"You could stay here," he said, looking down at his feet.

"As a slave?" I snapped back. I had thought better of him, but now I felt foolish and angry. Of course, I had to be of some benefit to him. He would not have come to rescue me for nothing. My mind leaped forward: he would sell me eventually, and then who knew who would own me or what would happen to me? No doubt an educated slave girl would make some money on market day.

"You could stay as a slave," he said bluntly. "Or you could stay as a wife."

I stop talking and give a short laugh. It's strange to think back on that day, though those words are imprinted on my mind like an official seal on a letter.

"So you did," you say, clearly uninterested in the love stuff.

"So I did," I agree. After all, there was not much love stuff, not at first.

You charge down the hill towards home, wooden spear whirling above your head. I watch you, smiling. You are right, of course. All that matters is that I am here. I stayed, as a wife, at the end of the Empire, where fate and the gods drove me.

Arcturus comes out of the house, a smile on his face at the sight of you back safely.

"Daddy!" You dismount and run into his arms. Arcturus hugs you and swings you around. He looks up at me. I raise a hand in a silent message: it is done. I have hidden the treasure until safer times come along.

For the truth is, Rome's Empire is over.

Looking back, I think the Empire began falling apart the moment that Septimius Severus died. He was the keystone that held the arch of the Empire together. Just six years after his body went up in flames on a hill near Eboracum, Julia Domna, Caracalla and Geta were all dead too. Caracalla murdered Geta, the army killed Caracalla, and Julia Domna took her own life when she knew that both her sons were dead.

I remember that eagle I saw soaring above Septimius Severus' funeral pyre. Back then, I thought it was the spirit of the Emperor. But perhaps it was the spirit of the Empire itself, leaving us – because things were never the same for Rome after that day. We were never really safe again.

179

The last emperor who was of Septimius Severus's line, Severus Alexander, has just been murdered by his own troops. There is no one to take the reins from him. Legions are arming and marching, and generals from Gaul to Syria, all wanting to be the next emperor of Rome, are preparing for war. It is vultures, not eagles, that will swoop on Rome now.

When Rome fights itself, the borders of the Empire will be left undefended. The Caledonians have never forgotten how Caracalla massacred their people. They will take their revenge on the Romans in Britain if they can, and we are in their path.

That is why I chose today to bury my treasures, the pieces of my story. They will remain hidden until times are safe again.

But, as I watch you play with your father, the wind scudding clouds high above our heads, I realise that I have buried another treasure today, one I did not plan to. I have buried the story of my life, the story of your history, in your memory. Some day, perhaps, you will dig it up – and pass it on to your children.

EPILOGUE

THE YORKSHIRE GUARDIAN

Saturday

ANCIENT TREASURE DISCOVERED
BY GIRL ON HOLIDAY

A silver 'treasure chest' dating to the third century AD has been discovered at Strandby Cliffs by a Birmingham girl on holiday in the area with her family.

Zaibun Ali (9) said: "I was just climbing on the rocks by the beach and I noticed something that looked like an old tin can, so I tried to get it out because we've been learning about keeping beaches clean in school. Then I saw that it was a box, and I showed it to my mum who said it was probably very old."

Researchers at the University of the North said that the engravings of Hercules and Dionysus on the sides suggest that the box was made in Leptis Magna, in present-day Libya. It would have belonged to a wealthy owner. They believe it dates to the reign of Septimius Severus, the first North African emperor of Rome, who ruled from York (then called Eboracum) from 209 to his death in 211 AD.

Dr Steve Smith, of the Department of Archaeology, said: "It's a bit of a puzzle, because the box is clearly meant for use as a medicine chest. It has the symbol of Asclepius, god of medicine and doctors, engraved on the lid – two snakes coiled around a staff. However, the contents are very varied."

The box contained a gold ring with an early Christian symbol on it, a bracelet made of jet from Whitby, and a small enamelled gold pot, which was probably intended for cosmetics. There was also some organic matter which has not yet been identified. It is thought it may have some connection with the ruins of a late second-century farm and villa some miles away, where skeletons of men, women and children from across the Roman world have been found buried.

Dr Smith commented: "Roman-era Britain was a

multicultural place. The Romans traded goods from as far away as China, so it is not a surprise that objects from Leptis Magna reached Britain. We just don't know the story behind this particular box."

The box may have been buried for safe-keeping during the so-called Crisis of the Third Century. In 235 AD, the last emperor of the Severan dynasty, Severus Alexander, was murdered and a chaotic time followed, in which the Roman Empire split into three parts, each controlled by a different general.

Zaibun said: "I want to be a doctor, so I was really excited to find out that the box was a medicine chest. But now I think I might want to be an archaeologist instead! I would love to know who buried the box and why."

The items will go on display at the county museum from September.

TIMELINE

193 AD/CE: The Year of Five Emperors. Septimius
Severus, a general in the army, comes
to power. Camilla is born. A severe fire
destroys much of the city of Rome.

207 AD: Camilla's family leave Leptis Magna for
Rome.

208 AD: Septimius Severus begins his journey to
Britain.

211 AD: Septimius Severus dies at York
(Eboracum)

228 AD: Camilla and Arcturus's son is born.

235 AD: The Crisis of the Third Century begins.
The last Severan emperor, Severus
Alexander, is murdered by his own soldiers.
Different generals fight for the Empire and
the Empire is eventually split into three.
The Roman Empire is never the same
again.

AUTHOR'S NOTE

When I was two years old, my family moved to Libya. I grew up in Benghazi. On weekends we sometimes went on long drives to the ruins of ancient Greek and Roman cities like Cyrene, where we played among fallen columns and picnicked with a view of temples.

I think this was where my love of history began. It was so easy to feel a connection to the ancient world when you were running around the same backyards and houses that children had run around over a thousand years ago. Of course, things had changed since the days of the Roman Empire, but some things were not so different. For example, the billboard-sized portraits of Libya's ruler, which were everywhere, were a lot like the arch of Septimius Severus.

As a result, it wasn't hard for me to imagine myself into Camilla's world. Nor was it hard to see that people have always travelled across the world, whether they wanted to or not, and created new homes, families and cultures wherever they went. All of these real people, for example, lived at around the same time that *Empire's End* is set:

- Septimius Severus: a Libyan-born emperor who died in York (Eboracum).
- The powerful Syrian wife of Septimius who followed him across the world, taking her religion with her.
- A Syrian called Barates who freed, then married, his British slave, Regina.
- The 'ivory bangle lady', found buried with rich jewellery in York. She had black African heritage and may have been a Christian.
- Galen, a Greek from Turkey, who became the most famous doctor ever. He treated emperors, including Septimius Severus – and invented the ham 'n' cheese treatment. (Yes, it's real. No, it doesn't work.)

Together, this group makes up a picture of a Roman world that was full of many different cultures, religions and ethnicities.

The Roman Empire, of course, was not paradise. It was a bloody, violent place, based on slave labour, where murder was entertainment and most women had little control over their lives. As soon as I introduced the fact that Camilla's family owned slaves (as they would have done in real life), I found I had to explore that in some way. I didn't feel comfortable ignoring the injustice of slavery, but nor did I feel comfortable pretending Camilla would have had the attitudes of a twenty-first-century person. I wanted Camilla to seem like a real girl, but a real *Roman* girl. As a result, slavery ended up being a bigger part of the book than I had first intended it to be.

In 235 AD, the year in which Camilla buries her treasure, the Roman Empire began to fall apart. When it was finally united again, it was as a Christian empire – a huge change from Camilla's world. Constantinople (today's Istanbul, in Turkey) became the centre of a new Holy Roman Empire. The city of Rome itself was overrun by invaders, and so were its provinces, including Britain. A world that people had thought would last forever had lasted just a few hundred years.

In the final chapter, Camilla is history and mystery for someone who will never know her story. The most interesting thing about history, I think, is that one day we will be history for someone else, in a world we can't imagine. How long will *our* world last? What treasures will we leave behind, and what will future historical fiction writers say about *us*?